WAR HANGOVER

A Novel by

GREGORY W. BITZ

ISBN: 0-944357-67-9
LIBRARY OF CONGRESS CATALOG CARD NUMBER 87-71864

FOR INFORMATION ADDRESS THE
PUBLISHER,
ANGEL WING PRESS, P.O. BOX 7586
MINNEAPOLIS, MINNESOTA 55407
PRINTED IN UNITED STATES OF AMERICA

LIMITED EDITION

MINNEAPOLIS
1987

WAR HANGOVER has been called many things. Experimental, too experimental, lyrical, far out, original, too full of truth. WAR HANGOVER is called a novel because the author says it is a novel. There are contradictions everywhere. WAR HANGOVER is a novel about war, but it is not a war book. Not a Vietnam book. Vietnam just happened to be the author's war. It is as timeless as it can be. It is full of truth and lies and life and death and love and weather and no love. There is a bunch of wisdom and a fair amount of humor. What is inside is what it is.

Other books by Gregory W. Bitz:
Fifty-five Leap Frogs, 1969
Parrot in the Wheat, 1971
Watch the Turtle, 1972
Dim Lake, co-authored, 1975
carrots, as we all know, do not cast shadows, 1977

The cover art and all drawings are by the author.

I respectfully dedicate this
book to Hollis Willeford, Yoko Ono,
and the memory of Ho Chi Minh.

and

To three children;
Mira in Germany
Hanna in Minnesota
Hanna in Germany

It is about finding peace.

Photograph by Stephen Boran

Gregory W. Bitz was a foot soldier
with the 4th Infantry Division
in The Republic of Vietnam.
He was shot twice in the taking
of Hill 1338 during the Battle of Dak To,
on November 17, 1967.
He is a graduate of, and a former instructor
at the Minneapolis College of Art and Design.
He lives somewhere in Minnesota.

I would like to thank the following people for their inspiration and assistance. Hollis Willeford, Tom Hennen, Mark Freeman, Maggie Molyneaux, Jeanne Alyce, C. A. Nobens, Jimmie Lee Coulthard, Lorenzo Milam, Patricia Hampl, Jonathan Sisson, Mary Easter, Larry E. Miller, Larry A. Thompson, Richard Shaw and the ever intuitive Gale Bailey.

My special thanks to Franz Allbert Richter for all his work designing and producing this book.

Ultimate thanks go to Katherine Van Kuluvar, my friend, agent and co-editor, without whose faith, help and advice this book would not have been published.

Gregory W. Bitz
July 1987
Minneapolis

CONTENTS

45. NEED.
HEADS BACK AND FORTH.
SEMANTICS.
SIZE OF A QUARTER.
46. TIRED.
HARNESS.
47. THOUGHT.
WAR CORRESPONDENT.
I, RESULT.
TOMBSTONE.
48. DEAD MEMORY.
IMAGINATION IN WAR.
YUP.
49. SMALL JUDGMENT DAY.
9.
TOMBSTONE.
50. MEMBERSHIP IS DOWN.
10.
11.
12.
13.
51. 14.
15.
CAN'T.
TURNER.
52. 16.
17.
18.
NIGHTMARE.
53. 19.
NO OLD MAN.
TOMBSTONE.
54. HESITATE.
TOMBSTONE.
FOREIGN STUDIES.
THE HIGHLANDS.
55. LITTLE WARNING.
20.
WORD GAME.
TOMBSTONE.
56. 21.
TOMBSTONE.
TOMBSTONE.

75. TRUTH.
44.
45.
76. FALSE HOPE.
46.
47.
77. 48.
49.
THE MONKEY HUNTER.
78. 50.
TOMBSTONE.
51.
79. 52.
53.
TOMBSTONE.
54.
80. OFFICIAL VISIT.
55.
TOMBSTONE.
81. 56.
57.
58.
TOMBSTONE.
82. 59.
60.
61.
83. TIRADE, TRIED.
84. 62.
HELP MUCH.
85. IN A FLASH.
63.
64.
TOMBSTONE.
86. THE WAR IN GENERAL.
THEY, THEM.
THE HOME FOR THE IRRETRIEVABLY FUCKED.
87. 65.
THERE LIES FAINT, WHITE AND EXHAUSTED.
88. DECEMBER 25.
TOMBSTONE.
89. SOME PEOPLE.
STATISTICS ARE IN.

115. TOMBSTONE.
74.
75.
76.
116. 77.
78.
THE HUMAN WAVE ATTACK.
117. 79.
80.
TOMBSTONE.
118. SHIFT AND SHINE.
IDEA.
SOMETHING TO THINK ABOUT.
119. THE BREATHING BASTARD.
THE FLIES.
81.
AMBUSH.
120. STRUNG UP, HANGING.
82.
TOMBSTONE.
TOMBSTONE.
QUESTION.
121. I THOUGHT I WAS ALONE.
123. I THOUGHT SOME MORE.
124. TOMBSTONE.
83.
TOMBSTONE, TO THE WIDOW.
LIGHTS WENT OFF, LEFT A GLOW.
125. 84.
TOMBSTONE.
TOMBSTONE.
TOMBSTONE.
126. 85.
86.
I SPAT STRAIGHT AHEAD.
127. TOMBSTONE.
WATER DOESN'T RHYME WITH LATER.
87.
INSIDE THE EARTH.
128. TOMBSTONE.
THE RAIN.
88.
CLEAN PLACE, CLEAN DAY.

129. 89.
TOMBSTONE.
90.
TOMBSTONE.
130. OLD LIGHTNING.
131. SETTLE ON IT.
132. 91.
92.
TOMBSTONE.
133. 93.
94.
95.
IT WAS A MURDEROUS MOSAIC.
TOMBSTONE.
134. 96.
BATTLEGROUND.
TOMBSTONE.
97.
135. 98.
99.
100.
DO YOU EVER.
101.
136. TOMBSTONE.
TOMBSTONE.
102.
SO I WAS WONDERING.
137. INTERPRET THIS.
TOMBSTONE.
THE VOICE RISES ON THIS ONE.
103.
138. TOMBSTONE
YOU ARE NOT WITHOUT FRIENDS.
104.
IT.
139. TOMBSTONE.
SORT OF HOW I FEEL.
105. ROUND.
106.

149. 125.
THE WHISPERERS.
126.
127.
150. TOMBSTONE.
128.
TOMBSTONE.
TOMBSTONE.
TOMBSTONE.
PART OF A POEM.
151. EVERYTHING IS ANSWERABLE.
TOMBSTONE.
TOMBSTONE.
TOMBSTONE.
BELIEF.
152. TOMBSTONE.
SOLVE THIS.
AFTERFIGHT.
YOU CAN WALK AROUND IT LIKE A LASER PICTURE.
153. FIRST.
SECOND.
TOMBSTONE.
THIRD.
154. 129.
130.
COME ON.
TOMBSTONE.
TOMBSTONE.
155. RECOVERY.
131.
OFF TO MY RIGHT.
TOMBSTONE.
156. WHEN.
TINY PRAYER.
132.
TOMBSTONE.
157. TOMBSTONE.
NICE IDEA.
133.
WISH.
WISH TWO.

158. I IMAGINE A FINE THING.
SOME THOUGHT ON DEATH.
TOMBSTONE.
159. KILLED SINGERS.
FACES IN THE TREES.
134.
160. WHY.
THIS.
135.
161. BREAKFAST.
HOW'D THEY KNOW?
REALLY PREENED.
136.
162. 137.
MOTHS.
163. REVERSAL.
TOMBSTONE.
138.
139.
140.
164. YOU MEET ALL KINDS.
165. FIVE PART PIECE.
1.
2.
3.
4.
5.
166. SIXTEEN TOMBSTONES IN A ROW.
TOMBSTONE 1.
TOMBSTONE 2.
TOMBSTONE 3.
TOMBSTONE 4.
TOMBSTONE 5.
TOMBSTONE 6.
TOMBSTONE 7.
TOMBSTONE 8.
TOMBSTONE 9.
TOMBSTONE 10.
TOMBSTONE 11.
TOMBSTONE 12.
TOMBSTONE 13.
TOMBSTONE 14.
TOMBSTONE 15.
TOMBSTONE 16.

168. I'VE BEEN A RAT.
CONFIRMATION.
TOMBSTONE.
169. SNAKES.
170. 2 ANIMALS.
TOMBSTONE.
TOMBSTONE.
141.
171. 142.
143.
144.
TOMBSTONE.
172. 145.
146.
THEM.
SICK.
173. WET COMPARISON.
CRASH.
147.
148.
174. 149.
AFTERNOON DISCUSSION.
150.
175. REMARKABLE.
FINALLY.
176. VIEW.
I KNOW THE HORROR.
MELANCHOLY.
177. YOU REMIND ME OF A MUSEUM.
151.
EYE ON YOURSELF.
178. YOUR WAR.
152.
153.
BAGGED ALIVE.
179. 154.
TOMBSTONE.
ROUGH EPITAPH.
FOREST NOISES.
155.

225. NOT YET.
re: TIME.
HOPELESS HOPE.
TOMBSTONE.
TO THE POINT.
226. CORRECTION.
THEY WOULDN'T ALLOW ME TO BE A BUDDHIST.
168.
169.
170.
227. 171.
HAPPY VALENTINE'S DAY.
228. YOU HAVE A CHOICE.
POEM.
TOMBSTONE.
TOMBSTONE.
TOMBSTONE.
229. HANDCUFFED IN THE VAGUE.
232. TOMBSTONE.
TOMBSTONE.
THE EVENIN'S COLOR.
COINCIDENCE.
233. DEAR BOB.
234. DID IT, EH?
235. REMEMBER, THIS IS A MELODIC FICTION.
236. A LIST FROM THEN.
237. NOW.
172.
173.
174.
238. 175.
THE KING OF SADNESS.
239. WHAT SAD WORDS THOSE ARE.
240. WITH A VIVID THRILL.
241. FEELS VERY BITTER AGAINST THE DEAD MAN.
242. THE AWE SYNDROME.
243. THE SNARE IS TOO PLAINLY SET.
244. FUNERAL DIRGE.
TOMBSTONE.
PATROL.

And the last of the sunlight is being hunted down
By something frozen.

Tom Hennen
1963

I. THERE IS A MOMENTARY HUSH.

NORMAN JAMES.

Norman James and I had smoked a lot together.
The very blue sky warmed up for our long
walk. The largest star I'd ever seen
was still but then vanished in the quick
sunburst.
We were always tired. But forced alertness
woke with us, like every other morning.
The huge leaves were wet usually. But
in the high hills, for some reason, dew
seldom showed. That was today. Somebody
said the thick trees kept the low level
dry, but I don't know, it sounds reasonable.
A bird flew out, the bush wavered. It
had a scissor tail. I wrote one person
about it already.
I liked that particular day. The moon
had been full the night before, and I
suppose I had a bit of moonstroke.
Some red ants bit into me while I sat
on vermiculated wood. I killed a few.
Norman James smoked almost constantly.
He killed a few too. It was fairly
quiet.

We all smelled bad. Bad odor was said
to repel mosquitoes, but it drew them
to us like a stinking magnet. Our
packs readied, we grouped for the start.
There was a lovely river nearby. We
were leaving it. Having bathed in it,
I knew I'd miss it. The first hill
tired me out. Vines were thick as we
went. I remember thinking of a name-
brand electric organ. That helped a little.
Once in a while the mountains were visible.
I wished to be there, they stood serenely.
But then we would be in a valley, seeing
only the thicket and huge trees. I hoped
for a blow dart to pierce my neck.
We thrashed through a leech-ridden pond.
More of the same and we finally stopped
for the night. I stripped to my shorts
and boots and began to dig our new apartment.
The sounds of chopping rang and the soft
thud of turning earth.

We finished and then ate. Some, in pre-
dusk defecation, rustled to our front.
Our defensive pie was finished. The
night went slowly. I woke up. It was
morning. Birds were awake too. There
were eleven full moons remaining if we
followed the plans. I smiled a lot even
then. Another full day of pathfinding,
we prepared for the coming night. Something
was wrong it seemed. Our water was good
but met with a lump in our every throat.
The sky grew grey and the trees took a
darker green. No sounds of nature, just
the clank of man.
I talked to Norman James before he went
out with the patrol. "It's always us,"
he said.
He was gone. Gunfire cracked and sputtered,
not long after, and men limped back. The
wounded cried and I felt sick. Norman
James didn't come back.

We spent the night. Morning kissed us
hello, and we all went out to destroy
the opposition. Jokes fell at our feet.
We knew we were in for it.
The climb was steep and loaded with fallen
trees. It was a real good day. The
ground was torn as though drunkenly plowed.
Death stench seemed to float at us from
the summit. Legs turned weaker, then
shaky. We waited for bullets. None came.
The hill was empty. The whole valley
was green. The grass, fairly wet from
ten minutes' rain, steamed. One bird
alone flitted up, then down. Maybe it
had returned home.

SHE KNEW.

I didn't know what was going on at first.
Then I saw the soldier get up smirking and
buckling up. A late teenager stood up.
The prettiest girl I had ever seen.
She started dressing, there must have
been fifty guys standing around. She had
the most unusual expression of victory
in her eyes and a set of lips that were
rigid and would never speak again. She
already knew the outcome of the war.

NOW.

Do you realize that right now, this very
instant, everything that could possibly
happen is going on?

1.

Using my imagination hardly restricts
my memory at all.

2.

There was a girl I saw who never became
famous. She was as old as she wanted
to be. Had you covered.
She honestly knew the nature of man.
She is still living, she must reappear
from time to time in future wars.

3.

It seemed that apart from self-control,
the best cure for pain was the pain of others.
That's probably not new.

REVERSAL.

So I got this idea. We sit around and wait for the N.V.A. prayers to make us go away. Fuck, we already know our prayers don't work.

AN OIL OF GLASS.

There's a picture from long ago of broken glass from a drink from long ago.

HIDE.

We came upon him maybe only a week after his eternal solitude was given him. His body was as if emptied. His head was out front, neck stretched. A grimace with open eyes. An extraordinary pelt.

DRIFTING IN THE WIND.

We got sleep to get.
To be dreaming into the wind. What do
you suppose happens to the dreams after
they have been drifting in the wind for
a couple of days? Busted up, or just hanging
loosely together. I wonder if they could
be regrouped and used again. These are
the dreams that were blown away before you
had them, by the way.

CLINK.

The lovely glasslike sound of thousands
of teeth flying around tinkling against
each other, and that little landing sound
like finches lighting on a pile of
sleighbells and slipping a little bit.

BRITTLE.

A lovely woman walked by us on patrol.
She sounded like running water. Then
a lovely old woman walked by. She
sounded like clear, cold, running
water, with light froth on it, like
there was a little bristling wind hitting
the tips of the waves. I wish you could
have seen that.

TOMBSTONE.

I got my strength from the storms and
the sunsets. Blah, blah, blah.

THE ELEMENTS.

Fire, phlegm, water, moonlight. At that
time of night, on that night, I was convinced
the world was, my world was, my world view was
made of the aforementioned.

4.

Caught in the middle of something I understand
perfectly. Man, is that scary.

5.

I was in the war before dope was invented.

WHAT A SHOW.

There was before us a lurid sunset.

TOMBSTONE.

One drumbeat somewhere.

APHORISM.

Death saved many marriages, strengthened many families, provided many excuses for temporary insanity.

6.

Many great loves died on the field. Many live on only for that reason. Millions of romances have been avoided through death.

BLACK TREES.

Black trees, they were in a drawing with
a white horse. It was, of course, a
visuality without precedent, completely
without reason. A queer beauty existing
only for its own sake, a pure existence.
Black trees, and somewhere back there,
a white horse.

TOMBSTONE.

I left directions for you, in case I
lose my mind, there's a baggage locker in...

7.

Called out with the low voice of deep
sleep. The lonely spirit inside.
Feigning happiness is rampant.

ANYBODY KNOW?

Were things in color two hundred years
ago? There are not as many references
to it in the things I have read. I have
the feeling there was more life in the
shade. Well, that's one thing I thought
about until the sun broke through the
high trees, the high slow trees.

8.

We go years without each other.
That weakens us. You are one of my
various sources of inspiration.

DARK PRODUCTION.

It came so often, so frequently, it
was always so deep and thick. It came
on and on. I'd blink and it would be
night. There was, I am sure, a night
factory somewhere underground. This could
be a dreamlike fiction. I'm not sure I
care. I think it is true. Can I not
have a first rate vision?

TOMBSTONE.

You can hear your life in your ears.
I could see it when I tilted my head back.

UNEXPECTED PLACES.

You could find this dark red decoration, like a fresco, a thick mix of blood and shellac all over the place. But oddly enough, never where you looked. Only on the bodies of the dead, in unexpected places.

IT FELT LIKE CLAP.

A bee flew in my nose and then flew
out my dink.

NOT WITH ME, I DON'T.

I find it difficult at times to coexist
with myselves.

MODEL.

I have become a central figure in some
rapidly executed imaginary paintings.

LIGHTED SEARCH.

There's something glowing in this niche.
A small busted heart with small thin
white roots looking for dirt.

RISK.

Stop looking into my eyes. (That's confidential.)
You will start, and I cannot afford, a
small light storm in there that could
render me weak of vision and vague
of motive. Turn on the dark, throw
the switch.

HE WAS COOL.

There was one guy from Jamaica or some magic spot. Puerto Rico, maybe. He didn't even have to be there. He couldn't stand it at home. Thought it would be a good way to make some money, he said. He was cool. He would just wave his hand for about five seconds when he was hot. A wind would start up. Bugs would be sucked away, his hair would blow, and all around, the other air was stagnant.

TOMBSTONE.

Waiting for you and your arrogant buddies.

TOMBSTONE.

The last kiss ever.

IT IS OVER.

Hey, come out of the foxhole.

WAKE THE FUCK UP.

If you would read or if you cared, you'd
know what precipice meant. 'Cause you're
on one, on the edge, a foot out in the air
and it's crumbling, and there are some
sharp rocks with open mouths below.

MAIL CALL.

I received a piece of ham in the shape
of Minnesota which I would not eat
which I have kept safely in my pocket
all these years.

SEVERE DEFECTS.

The bastard had so many affectations
he looked like a wood carving.

I LOOK DOWN AND ASK.

How much of me is me.

NEED.

I felt as though I needed some kind of
weird clairvoyant. Is a clairvoyant
ever not weird.

HEADS BACK AND FORTH.

After looking up at their fortifications,
I saw their helmet tops. Looked like
the fastest goddamn turtles I ever saw.

SEMANTICS.

A tawdry pigment of our past, or is
that tawny?

SIZE OF A QUARTER.

Going home? That's not any weirder than
wanting to go to the moon. The fucker
is only this big.

TIRED.

Always on the move. Constant motion. Kissing's difficult when you're running. Sleeping on the run is rough on your face. God, it would be decent to rest in one place. I wonder why I do it. I can't imagine why. There's something in my brain that drives me on. I've got to keep moving. I hope you understand. It'll probably stop soon. I can't go on forever. Then we can talk and sit with tea. Everything good is just over the hill. Just a foot beyond where your vision stops. An inch out of reach, an hour away. A short week off. Around the corner. In that shallow dark hole we call the soul. But I can't walk that far.

HARNESS.

Harness the rage.
Use it for power.
Maybe run an electric plant.
Let's go clean the gun
and go to bed.

THOUGHT.

It was a notable morning. Her breath
smelled like dreams. She exhaled. Here
are the bags full of night you ordered.
Here are the baskets of shadows. Here,
too, the jars of grim thought.

WAR CORRESPONDENT.

So, then, I looked in the viewfinder and
what to my bewilderment and utter astonishment
a flaming water buffalo is cruising
toward me bellowing, on second thought,
screaming. I give out the loudest halloo
money can buy, chuck the Nikon, and
hightail it straight back to Saigon.

I, RESULT.

I have become a culmination of my own
durability and duality.

TOMBSTONE.

I heard through the grapevine the trees
are all insomniacs.

DEAD MEMORY.

I'll always remember that day. It started out so still. We were just doing some regular things. Some people in the hills still don't know what happened. Everything turned so blue. I'll always remember that. It happened so fast. It was so dreamlike but there's the proof. We will always remember, you can kill us, too. You can kill us now.

IMAGINATION IN WAR.

The two are inseparable. Your mind is constantly inventing. You know so much, but are so uncertain about it all. Millions of shadows were killed. Oddly, thousands in hand to hand combat.

YUP.

Just think of this. Anything that you can think of happened. Go ahead, invent one. Yup. Ask anybody.

SMALL JUDGMENT DAY.

Lying, mouth open, looking like a poor
dead idiot, hands out in supplication.
A pile of noisy green parrots overhead
questioning that pose.

9.

I guess after all these years, I should
open my eyes and accept other approaches
to this aftermath. If you want to cry
and whine and drink and be fucked up,
of course that is your own way. Maybe
somebody will learn something from that.
If enough people see how fucked up so
many people are, that could have as much
effect against war as the fear of death.
Who knows, maybe enough people will think,
if this keeps up, we'll have a population
of drunken whiny old men. Something
I'm not going to look forward to. I'd
rather live alone in an old Chevy
eating pain pills and bein' quiet. Talkin'
to the radio.

TOMBSTONE.

God, there was so much obvious stuff.

MEMBERSHIP IS DOWN.

The secret order of the you know what.

10.

I wish I was something else. I am my own fantasy. The hard part is being somebody elses'.

11.

After he put a bullet in his head, here is the note we read:
"I've changed my mind."

12.

A day of contrasts.

13.

We're living on the edge of several things, yesterday, for example.

14.

Do you suppose any new colors were developed
as a result of this whole war business?
If so, any we would want to use in our
work? Any suitable for clothing?

15.

It was clear as the nose off his face.

CAN'T.

It, well, you cannot describe it. Because
there is a meaning there that has no sound.

TURNER.

During an evening gunfight, the sky had
a beautiful cast. The rice and bamboo
were shiny and blue. A field of flax on
fire.

16.

I just gave myself a good mindreading.

17.

Some of these fucking commanders are hemosexuals. They like blood, I mean really like it.

18.

I'm a tramp. Goddamn it. You caught me again.

NIGHTMARE.

I'm so glad it isn't me. Something moaned in another room. She was hard of hearing, only heard what she wanted to hear.

19.

How many wake up to the sound of their
own whining, alarmed at the amount of
noise your dreams make.
A grim, terrible something.

NO OLD MAN.

Think of all the great 12 year old kids
who are not around. Just look around.
I bet there were at least two children
who did not just walk by because their
fathers couldn't seem to get off the ground.

TOMBSTONE.

It was a big green mess.

HESITATE.

It was a funny mixture of fear and excitement.
I hestitate to call it a "unique blend".

TOMBSTONE.

We walked along with a fool in our hands.

FOREIGN STUDIES.

Death is quite an education, sometimes.
It was a notable morning. I like to
think of it as forced dreaming. Not
all the time of course, that would
be an extreme. It may sound square,
but it was a son of a bitch sometimes.

THE HIGHLANDS.

Give it the green star, decorated for greenery.

LITTLE WARNING.

Well, before you go out and get killed,
or fucked up, I thought you'd like to
know, war is only really bad. So don't
say I didn't tell you. I don't want to
hear you say, "God, I didn't expect this."

20.

The guns as greedy and misguided as the
man who ordered them fired.

WORD GAME.

Put the letters D E A D on a page and
move them around. You can spell dead
two times, or four, if you have a southern
accent...DAED, and DADE.

TOMBSTONE.

Remember more things, this would be good.

21.

You know, people have been going to their deaths accidentally, knowingly, willingly, stupidly, for thousands of years. I'm not telling you anything new. Oh no. You know this, everybody knows this, except, it seems, the people who can prevent it. So what's the deal?

TOMBSTONE.

The opening wind, a real brainstorm. Everything is acceptable.

TOMBSTONE.

Memory. Something stuck in my mind.

GOOD NAMES.

The mountain people had names for them.
Like: the flower that resembles a bee,
the flower that cries one tear only,
the flower that thrives on sun and frequent
visits.

22.

I realized I was parked real far away.

23.

Unmen, send me magic, have a person to
send me magic.

24.

My mind was so hot. I stay alive by
warming my hands over my head.

RESPITE.

I'll just sit down and die for a little while.
I ain't gonna do it anymore.

TRY THIS.

Reading by treelight, baumlicht.

25.

Ad lib gunfight. Glib fun gunfight.

26.

He screamed enthusiastically, your
manhood's on the line,
he said euphemistically.

27.

The screaming earth.

28. SCAR.

Carrying this around for years. Using it as a co-star.

29.

Yikes. The smoke slowly dissipated and then rapidly was sucked down into a small hole.

30.

I am sure a sheltered life killed a lot of people.

BACK.

I dreamt way back. The heat was ferocious. She was almost frozen. Near death, she said. I loved her twisted sense of drama. A master of exaggeration. She dug foolin' with me, sometimes she'd fool when she was in trouble. I think she lost her mind that winter. She looked great in that snowstorm. I wish I had known what to look for. Maybe she would be around now. Who knows?

TOMBSTONE.

Time in memory.

TOMBSTONE.

It is hot. I am absolutely passionless.
Well, that could be a lie.

CORRECTION.

It just doesn't work like that.

31.

When the war broke out (for me)
I went to all my favorite places I'd
never see again, I'd never see them again.

SOME NAMES.

Sometimes, when I hear my own name, it
sends chills up or down my spine. The
direction is neither predictable nor
important. There are some names I cannot
even hear anymore. I will not permit
some of them into my ears. Some names
uttered by parrots or whimpered would
boil blood. I will not mention them.
They foul the eye and ear.

32.

Why is art so frightening to the government?

FACE TO FACE.

It can take years to unravel what happened and what you did. Once the answer is clear, once you attain the freedom from those years, when things seem, that's <u>seem</u> perfect, we try to kill the thing we have become. It is very mature. It is nature. It has been around a long time. And it grows, and learns things, just like, or similar to, a dangerous dog.

33.

It certainly underscored the need to live.

THE DAY WENT SILENT.

From aviary to tomb. The leaves stopped
rustling, they even knew a storm was coming.
Birds dropped down. Down from treetops,
from low branches, from small rocks. All
dropped down and flattened against the
earth. A result of good training. For
moments, long, long moments, the day was
stopped. Except for a cough now and then
from a bonehead, there was nothing to hear.
The farm boys knew something right away.
I was half-farmboy. Half something else.
Then it came. Nobody heard it but me.
A long high note, associated with suspense.
It was unmistakenly unmistakably a violin.
Played with the devotion of a master.
A note that has been practiced and played,
unaltered for years, perhaps centuries.
A note one man had played exclusively
for this moment. His day had finally come.

So had ours. All hell broke loose. The
dam broke, the sky opened up, the wind
blew, birds died of fright, just like
they were supposed to. Flightless destiny.
Trees keeled over, the sun went out, the
moon came up. All the oceans jumped.
Every grandmother's teacup on earth
cracked or shattered where it stood.
Hanging, on a shelf, or in midsip.
Bulls, perplexed, humped electric fences.
Bombs were falling on Hanoi in such
numbers that I wouldn't believe anyone's
story. Every dandelion on earth went to
seed and went up like a magnificent puff
of smoke. The signal went unseen by most
of the world.

Those of us who did see it have either
been assassinated or are dying of cancer.
There will be no investigation. Because
I'm certainly not going to mention it.
Because either I'm dead, or those guys
across the street will have me by six.
And they have ways of making your tongue
not work, and your voice go dead.

WELL, I DID NOT WANT TO BE ALL ANIMAL.

Delirious, that's what we were. Look
that up. No, I'll do it for you...
You become part animal. It depends
on something what animal. Or you become
parts of lots of animals. Small parts, big
parts, small parts small animals, and
so on. You choose, sometimes. Other
times, you get chosen. Sometimes how you
look helps determine which animal you
become. But mostly it's how you act.
Often, if the animals take over, you look
more like them than you do. Confused?
Some try to be bigger than they can be.
Some become as small as they want to be.
Able to hide, climb, disappear. Some
are always visible, as if that is primary.
I think I was a tired Shetland pony
who wanted to be a shooting star...
Well, I didn't want to be all animal.
Delirious, that's what we were. Look
that up, no, I'll do it for you.

THE BLOWN UP GUY.

We got to watch it from the very beginning.
The mortar round hit right behind and
under him. At first, you go through
all the mental stuff. The Oh My Gods
and the Jesus Christs, the Holy Fucks,
the Oh Nos. All that stuff. You can
get a lot out in a short time. You
remember all the times you got drunk
and got laid together. Odd, is it not?
<u>His</u> life flashes before <u>your</u> eyes. So
does his death. Everything happens so
fast, they tell you. That's true. But
if you really concentrate, you can piece
it together visually while it's happening.
First, the ground goes up and your
friend becomes part of a big cloud.

He looks like he is starting to do a
jumping jack. That is when it speeds
up. You can't afford to blink now.
You owe him this. Wide-eyed you see
his gear get out of the way. Clothes
shred. Then your eyes meet.
And I caught a faint smile, a glint of
his everlasting humor and a brilliant
instant thumbs up as he went gone.

IMPAIRAMOUR.

Sometimes I do not have successful
relationships. This could be due to my
insanity, or maybe because I don't trust
anybody anymore. Doesn't matter. I can
read.
Shortly after I told her I had received
my draft notice, I received a rejection
notice from her. There is some time
needed to figure that one out. I'm
going to war, not you. Oh, I get it,
YOU don't want to run the risk of wasting
a year on somebody who may not love you
when he gets back. Or is it that there
is no point in putting that much time in
on a dead man. Well, I understand.
Doesn't matter. I can read.
Funny how nobody wants to go to bed with
a man who's going to war. I'm not
going to die on you for Christ's sake.
I have enough class to wait until I
go into combat. I suppose it would
give you the creeps to have slept with
a dead man. Just think, kissing those
dead blue lips. God, Betty, he's dead.
And I slept with him last September.
Oh, ick.

34.

Was he aware of his own safety?

TOMBSTONE.

Down at water's edge.

TOMBSTONE.

I now give her something only I can provide.

WET AMBUSH.

Water dripping on hard leaves sounds like fingernail clippers snapping. How many fingers? Which is worse, listening to rain drops for seventeen straight hours or somebody cutting their nails for that amount of time?

35.

The swine song of a girl and a soldier.

TOMBSTONE.

It seems that now we can get some definition
of random.

36.

Every time I take a walk there's fog
on the street. A grey line a foot high.

37.

Walkin' amongst a giant living Rousseau.

A GREAT WONDER.

One night, when the air was clear, there came a soft sound that we could not hear. You had to see it. It was albino bats. Backlit by the stars. The harder you looked, the louder it was. This became tiresome after an hour, after hour after hour. They sensed this and flapped away. Well controlled bunch. You can imagine what that looked like. Blind, albino ideas. Been in the dark so long they came out squinting.

38.

He used to say he would give his left nut.
Well, he finally did.

39.

Well, I still have the rest of my life.

40.

There was a shot and a scream, he hit every note in between. What a solo.

41.

I close my eyes and I see the rats run across my nose.

WHEN.

Well, I'm all grown up now. When's it gonna hit me? Life's direction I mean. You know, the money, the jobs, the sense of success, the scent of happiness. Goddamn it, I'm past 25. What's gonna happen, and when? I'm ready for everything except nothing.

42.

The guns went deaf. They could not hear the cease-fire order.

43.

He couldn't make those things occur. He just simply could predict coincidences. Sometimes you can make things happen.

TRUTH.

It has been my experience that lying
is a very important means to getting
to the truth.
I think that is called intelligence
gathering.

44.

You've got Vietnam written all over you.
Oh yeah, thanks, you look crazy too.

45.

Some days I wake up and it feels like my
heart has fallen asleep.

FALSE HOPE.

Bullets leave such big holes. Somebody said that. He begged for a snake. He's probably begging in New York now. Hey, buddy, got any spare snakes?

46.

Ah, the bastards have finally become unmasked. False hope.

47.

Often, in order to complete an unsavory deed, you need a negative incentive. Like being shot in the back. Or would not being shot in the back be a better example?

48.

Whenever there was a real chance to think there came a puking sadness.

49.

Sit around not knowin' stuff.

THE MONKEY HUNTER.

I guess first you should know where to look. And then you should find a place to hide and change. Dress up like a bush. Or maybe you should go through the brush real loud so the monkeys think you are not thinking about them. Then when you get a good view of one of the closer ones, shoot him for Christ's sake. Then I suppose you have to decide what to do with a dead monkey. Oh, I can think of 50 uses right off the bat.

50.

I got a postcard from my last battlefield
it was written weakly like with a broken
hand and an empty pen and a shaken belief
an old weird dead vibration.

TOMBSTONE.

Looking for a reason for coming here.

51.

Imagine a twenty year old shithead thinking he knew more than I know. I grew up with the Chinese. See, you must get into their heads. To do this you must eat their food. Yup. Take it right off their plates. This way you get fed and earn their respect. You learn a lot, I tell you, watching. Just look at their language. You've really got to be smart to understand that crap.

52.

Excuse me, can't talk, lost my voice
in the war. And I'm sorry, my cock
was blown off too. Luckily, I did not
lose my manhood or have my sense of
humor shot off.

53.

A long life was not always a result
of worthwhile independent thought.

TOMBSTONE.

Mad little creature.

54.

There was shown sufficient pathos.

OFFICIAL VISIT.

Jesus, Buddha, Mohammed, Jehova, Krishna, Brahma, Manitou, Confucious, Lao Tzu; all the big guns showed up disguised as a Swiss observation group. They deemed it a fair struggle. They remarked that everything was going as planned, and should continue. Let's see what happens.

55.

He shouted the perfect no. He yelled a perfect no.

TOMBSTONE.

He kept on. He persisted in his dreary dream.

56.

His hand looked like a crab on a stick.

57.

He gave one of those scrunched up little
waves that children give, and you give back.

58.

I did a backflip into myself. Learned
a great deal, but that was to be implied.

TOMBSTONE.

I wear the medallion of the saint of distrust.

59.

Like being in the French Foreign Legion, down to the last second, we were throwing words, literally. That really puts a dent into a human wave attack.

60.

Yes. I have spit on paradise, I have often said no.

61.

I felt bad, I couldn't help it. I felt bad. I couldn't avoid it. It got into bed with me last night. I woke up and bad was all over me. I ran to the store hoping to shake it. I showered again. I felt bad. I felt real bad. I made some calls to all my friends. But they complained of the same thing, more or less. For the first time I was glad I was not alone. We all feel bad. That's good.

TIRADE, TRIED.

A huge problem is that we treat the death of a soldier as a shame, a dreadful loss. True, it is a loss. But if we were to treat the death as the GLORIFIED thing that it once was, we could dispense with so much GRIEF. Soldiers are supposed to die, it's what they're for. At least on one side, anyway. Some are to enjoy surviving (our side) but they also should know that they are to someday join the dead. When you accept the reality that it does not hurt to die, you can go out and be a great fighter. And, if it were not for the insane fears of the so-called Unknown thrust upon us by the twisted minds of the church, no matter which church, many other grim things could be avoided. Like silly GUILTS. Go with God, my son. Thank you, Padre, but could I have a few thousand more rounds too? Want to come along?

62.

Living in the west, a disorientation.

HELP MUCH.

You might want to consider the possibility
that your youth was in large part to
blame for what you now feel. In youth
there are holes in your intellect. Holes
that take years to fill. That is what they
count on, see? They will not help us now.
They won't even explain it to us. Excuse me
while I fill a little hole. It is up to you
and us to understand what happened and realize
that we fell into a well laid trap. Maybe
the only way we can help those who did not
get out of it is to reveal now what we learned.
And how we fell for it. I've got to go get
some more hole filler now.

IN A FLASH.

A flash light a firelight a flashfight
a firefight a flare light flash fight
night fire fight a night sight flash frame
freeze frame flare sight fire fight a
quick sick snap flash flesh fight night fight
phosphorus flare flash in flash out get in
get out flight this is not right firefight.

63.

We succeeded despite a spasm of unfettered panic.

64.

Yes, it is my intention to do the thing you mentioned.

TOMBSTONE.

Beneath this heart of blond there beats
a heart of grey.
Beneath this grey stone there beats a
heart that stopped. Stopt.

THE WAR IN GENERAL.

Thank god I won't live to remember this.

THEY, THEM.

Do they really "melt" into the underbush?
Does the jungle "swallow" them up?

THE HOME FOR THE IRRETRIEVABLY FUCKED.

Some kind of grey lair, that's what it seemed like most all the time, but misty on the mostly rainy days when you couldn't get a straight thought out of your own head if you paid yourself. Hmmm, a hiding place in your own head. What a strange place. If they found you, they would find your hiding place. If you burned it, your own head would go up. But perhaps that is what started the whole thing anyway.

65.

Yes, it was genuine gunfire. With bullets in it and everything.

THERE LIES FAINT, WHITE AND EXHAUSTED.

Eye catching death brutally beautiful. Contempt for the rainbow more colorful than a barrel of colors. The trees were white. Either from fright or loss of blood. Some of them, a sickly pink, were deep red on the bottoms. This from soaking up the blood from the ground. There, on the crest was a small herd of red horses. Bright red horses. Standing quietly, waiting, nipping some grass, or who knows, maybe grazing on flowers. Who knows what spirit horses eat? Well, untie me, and I'll go find out.

DECEMBER 25.

Think of your work as a story. Embellish it,
put color to it, it can be simple or it can
be elaborate. Is this your first spell?
What were the other ones like, how many
spells did you cast on him? Stop looking
into my eyes, this is confidential. Is it
possible to come <u>up</u> from the deep edge?
Think of your life as a story. Color it.
Color it any way you want to. Cover it
with mud. Sharpen it with a knife. End it
with a song. Attach it to a kite. Tie it
to a wren, bite it like a pear, wipe it off
the floor, lock it in the cellar.

TOMBSTONE.

Save your breath, lover, you're talking
to a memory.

SOME PEOPLE.

Some people still stand or sit in front of their windows looking out. I do not think it means anything beyond that. Also, some people enjoy finding faces in clouds or in the shadows. I still do this and do not consider it odd. There are many things to see, from the windows, in the shadows, in the clouds. There are faces in the windows across the street. There are clouds in their heads and shadows on the faces. I see nothing odd about that.

STATISTICS ARE IN.

Do you realize that more magic and spells and poetry and incense and prayers and invocations were used in this war than in all other wars combined except that one war we had in the early fifties?

THE DOOR GUNNER.

Had a view. Rained down diamonds. Looked through rivers, saw the bottom of the world. Saw the top from the other side down. All the green they saw is still in their eyes. They wake up with diamonds near them, after dreaming about other things they do not reveal. They see the world and do not say much.

TOUGH TO BELIEVE FOR SOME OF YOU.

We could smell the N.V.A. It was one of the most interesting odors imaginable. We knew they were around, or had been. But our ones in charge didn't smell well, or they were really into cologne. It seemed like a thick yellow fog, their smell. They ate differently. They smoked funny cigarettes, and their fires were not like ours. Their camps smelled like witches and spirits lived there and kept camp. Maybe even cooked for them. But if we couldn't have witches, why should they? We could afford some very high witches.

THE NORTH VIETNAMESE SOLDIERS' PRAYER.

Dear Lord, thank you for our meagre
supper to sustain me in the upcoming
battle with the American Skyrats, and
the disgusting yet brave, ground adversary.
I will admit some fear and hope you will
understand if I duck once in awhile.
We are doing a bad thing and I think
we should return home. Yes, the
American Dogs should leave here, but
we have been real pricks, too. Time
will right things. There is plenty of
that. I will fight to the death as will
my comrades. But I wish to go on record
as saying that, despite my deep devotion
to homeland, and to you, Oh Generous and
Vivid Entity, I am playing along
under protest. I want to own a store
some day, I am out of cigarettes, and there
are no chicks here. Amen.

SOMETHING STILL LINGERS.

We must keep our sense of history sharp. Right now I am holding my father's dog tags. EDWIN H. BITZ
37278597 T42-43 A
ALMA M. BITZ c/o ANDREW AARSTAD
DAZEY N. DAK P
He was a soldier at Normandy. He never spoke of the war in Europe. Except I remember he said that once the bees were so thick that they ate them with their K-rations. He lived through that too. But he was very quiet. He laughed when he had to. It is now longer since I was in combat than it was for him when I would pump him for answers. I would try to get the whole cool story. He would say it was pretty tough, that the country was beautiful and that the people were nice. He made a lot of friends, he said.

Sounds like the same war to me. We
drank ourselves to death and back many times.
I have no idea how much we are alike or
how we are different. I'll never know
for sure, anyway. Exactly a year before
I was shot, a couple bottles of vodka
slipped down his throat and killed him.
Infiltrated the lines like a couple of
sappers, caught him off guard and cut his
throat. He was a fine man, a good soldier
and he died in the weirdest combat of all.

NEW THING TO SEE.

Seeing the sky for the first time.
That flickering cheap blue rained
drops of blood. Some stars fell too.
I stayed up all night justifying it.
I wear black once a year to remember,
so I'll probably go nuts. Now is the
time before the edges of our lives
turn brown. I don't agree with those
who say we're running out of time. I
say we have just enough.

TOMBSTONE.

Lavish use of lunacy.

TOMBSTONE.

I don't wanna die. I just got born.

LIGHT CAST LIKE A SMALL LANTERN.

Or a baton of yellow light. It laid
there glowing up some sticks and night
bugs. Not very dramatic, but I guess
some things are meant to be simple.

lowercase tombstone.

anything else you should know?

THERE IS HOPE.

Somtimes, you just feel ruined. You're really not. You're just as hot as you ever were. You just need to eat more eggs for your coat, you know, get your shine back.

RAMBLE.

The smells limped along the jungle trail
leaving a weak trail. Some of us reach
the top of the hill. Everybody sits
down. I want to go on. It was with this
falseness of purpose that I entered into
this liaison. Clothed for subterfuge,
love as a weapon. Before I personally
die, I want to say, with perfect split
vision, that I am not a dancing bear.
I'm the guy who invented sunshine. Where
is the guy who made the rain and cold?
We'll, he didn't make enough.

TOMBSTONE.

I'm down here. It's a frightening thought.
I don't want to water it.

A TABLEAU, A MOVING ONE.

We were lying there in bed an instant after furious lovemaking. We both were almost senseless. I was on top. Next I was very comfortably positioned in a shallow pit on a high hill overlooking a deep ravine which went up again to a high, fairly steep incline. It looked like an eighty degree angle from where I was. About three hundred yards away. I saw them right away. I didn't count them until later. At that moment they were just a bunch of N.V.A. trying like fuck to get up a hill. And it looked like tough climbing. Two just got to the top as this scene started. One stood up straight to look the place over.

The other bent over to help the third one who was quite close. He had a mortar base plate on his back and no rifle. The one bending over had two rifles. The man on top, one. I took as much time as I thought I had sighting in the leaning man. I dropped him with the first shot. The top man stopped stunned and looked around some. He surprisingly crouched and bent over the top of the hill and reached out to the third man. I carefully put a round squarely on his back. The base plate stopped it, but he slid a few feet back. I shot once more. The round fell a foot below his feet. I brushed her hair away. I raised the barrel and put the next round in the back of his head, and he stopped like he was nailed to the ground. Then he started sliding again. Slowly at first, and then his feet hit a root and he pitched backward.

Topheavy, he dropped into the fourth man.
He held on as Baseplate went by him.
The man on top had disappeared into the
green. I wiped off my face and glasses
and dug my elbow into the bed. The fourth
man stopped to turn around and took the
round in the chest. Nailed to the hill
for an instant, he then slipped and dropped
his rifle. He came to rest on the shoulders
of the next man down, who, I expect, was
dismayed. Men six, seven and eight tried
to retreat down the hill with their gear.
They had a barrel and some mortar rounds,
plus their rifles. I hit number eight
as he hit the base of the hill. Mr.
Seven tried to run down the hill, but
it was more of a dive, and he landed on
his face. I dropped him as he rose to
his knees.

This left the man in the middle plodding
down and sideways, hand over hand, his
head turning back and forth, or side to
side. A hill climber waiting for a bus.
Two rounds suddenly kicked up to my left.
The man on the top had come to his senses.
I put my gun on automatic and emptied
my clip into a bush. There. Nothing
more happened. The other guy was creeping
into the open and heading for some short
trees. I reloaded and shot him in the
leg. She woke up and said, "How many
did you get?"

SOME TRUTH TO THAT.

Some people stay drunk for years to avoid
being a disappointment.

TOMBSTONE.

Poor judgment.

GIRLS.

In native dress walked away resembling
kites drifting straight down the path.

NOT THIS DREAM.

I never got to fight in the open for
an old French farmhouse dodging and
flirting with well aimed rounds hitting
the real dry dirt of Europe using all
the guile I'd kept in escrow to get
close and pick off a Nazi and drop
him from seventy yards. Something I
had always wanted to do.

THIS DYING BUSINESS REQUIRED SOME THOUGHT.

The order of it was reasonably fascinating. First choice of weapons, or was that third? and lastly, there was whether you wanted death badly enough. Oh, sure, sometimes you did not get a <u>real</u> choice. But there were times when you could die or not.

INFANTRY CHARGE.

Bein' in one. Think about that for a minute.

ROCK'S IN MY HEAD.

I got up and felt like a bad guitar solo.

66.

Ever seen a watermelon plastered all over the road? Well, there were some things over there that brought that image to mind.

67.

I think I've been swindled again.

BRING 'EM BACK ALIVE, WHY?

This would be unreadable if it was completed. It would be vile, and the description of what I have in mind would really make a lot of you sick. It is a very delicate subject and there are so many hopes that cannot be fixed. Believe me, I would barely be able to get through it.

VARIATION ON
THE "TWO LEADERS FIGHT IT OUT" IDEA.

Why didn't congress just appropriate
the funds for an international drinking
contest? Australia, Korea, and us. Plus
some of the reporters. Against them.
I could have put together a team that
would have either restored the peace
or made Gettysburg look like a picnic.

IN YOUR LIFE.

What do you usually do when it gets dark?
Does a candle usually work?

68.

If it ain't there, it's gone.

BATTLEGROUND.

It was slippery. Like the stretch of
road after a toad run and a hundred cars.

DENT.

I must have been way out of range, because
when the bullet hit me, it only dented
me. Just like when my sister used to
squeeze my arm when she was pissed.

69.

I jumped in front of myself to see if
I was still there.

70.

They tried very hard to omit me from
my future.

71.

Considering the ways I have been, will you please omit me from now on?

72.

You know, you're always runnin'. Trying to beat the dark.

QUIET, NOW.

Hey, shut up you two. You two, yeah, you. You're bleedin' too loud. Quit that gurgling, knock off that groaning. Die more like two butterflies.

73.

I never go into detail anymore.

MY LOST ART.

I keep talking so fast, fragmented. Thoughts
unfinished. I think I want to get it over
with because I think nobody will be listening,
or nobody will be there to listen by the
time I'm done. I can tell a whole story
in about a minute. And you will walk
away commenting on the way my eyes scan
the world from top to bottom. And probably
how I seem to want to be somewhere else.

NOVEMBER 6, 1967 TO JON WELCH.

Two cats, wild, came near. I would have
watched them longer but I got up quickly.
I've been nervous the past six days.
I guess they were too.

II. THERE IS A LULL, A PAUSE.

You dream yourself into something
and then must fight your way out.

AUGUST 13, 1967 FORT PUKE, LA.

Dear Ma,
Hello, the day is good. I'm in the library's peacefulness. I'm sorry to hear you missed your bus. Did you take the spectacles in, dear? I hope so, so I'll have them to wear. Civilian ones don't fit anymore and my army ones are too attractive.
We got back from "Tiger Ridge" Saturday. It was blister-style hot all week, until Friday night. We have moved out of our barracks and are living in tent city. Which is just that. Seven man tents. We do have an outdoor shower (next to the road) 2 latrines with 4 stools (to accommodate 190 men) and a half mile to walk to the mess tent now.
Oh, I got a wonderful thought. If you haven't taken the glasses in, have him lightly tint them rose. Yours sonnily,
Bitz.

FIRST IMPRESSION.

The first dead man I saw was made of
brick. A stray round hit him while he
was talking. That alone is out of place.
You just don't stand around and get shot
for good. So I did a splendid portrait
of him with large facsimiles of his
several corpulent lovers kneeling over
him in uncontrollable grief. The two
essences, those of death and grief were
at their best in this work. Death laid
there. The painting heaved periodically.

HE WAS NOT DIM IN THOUGHT.

Help me, I'm hit.
Just slow in speech.

TOMBSTONE.

They kept us scared and stupid.

74.

But now he was really dead. And man, would the girls mourn.

75.

I only could think of his two fat lovers. He talked constantly about them. They were fat. Not very fat, or extraordinarily fat, or immense. They were fat. Fat was enough for him. It was it.

76.

The first dead man I saw was made of brick.

77.

He was in such a frenzy after the fight he fell down fast and fucked a puddle of blood.

78.

Let the pigs run wild. They are heading for the mine field. Finally, the pig is useful.

THE HUMAN WAVE ATTACK.

What an image. I didn't think of it like that so much when I was there. It was just a term that was used for some thing horrible. Like a banzai attack. But when you think of a wave comprised of humans. Coming straight at you. Falling, and rising, some of them going high, cresting and then falling and being lost with new ones taking over. Substitute water. Of course there is an end to it. Whether you are there to see it is another story. But whether you see it or not, there is a big dead human wave at twelve o'clock low.

79.

Almost fell down, almost died. Almost fell into the warren of deepness.

80.

In a way, when they attacked in force straight at you, and you fired at them (in force) they gave their lives and took them at the same time. It was a moving firing squad situation.

TOMBSTONE.

Those hordes of khaki walked into my life and walked into their death.

SHIFT AND SHINE.

The flies and bees shifted quickly in flight. So quickly that they'd send off reflections so fast, like the shine on shoes or the gleam off a top hat. It was like fightin' flying mirrors.

IDEA.

I had a platoon of woodpeckers. I cleared it with my "superiors". They liked the idea. "Woodpeckers," they said, "sounds good." I waved them on into battle with the "forward ho" of older days.

SOMETHING TO THINK ABOUT.

The vague elements of the enemy.

THE BREATHING BASTARD.

Nobody ever caught him. Only a few
of us know who he was. Both of him.
They don't need recognition. They got
what he wanted.

THE FLIES.

Feed, that's really all they do. Sit
around and feed in the same spot, forever.

81.

Get all freaky and historical.

AMBUSH.

I waited from head to toe.

STRUNG UP, HANGING.

I'm suspended, between everything. Between black and white, wrong and right, up and down, smile and frown, hate and love, below and above, name it and claim it.

82.

There was an old dream, lying on the ground.

TOMBSTONE.

I'd like to invite you into my world.

TOMBSTONE.

They, the dead, are living proof.
The one I get to look at most.

QUESTION.

What did they call shellshock a thousand years ago? Swordshock?

I THOUGHT I WAS ALONE.

See, part of the reason it's taken
so long to crack is that most of us are
soldiers. Still soldiers. We fight.
We fight everything that fights us.
Especially this, because we can't really
see it. It is there, we see it in others
or read about it. We even see it in
ourselves, but it's hard to fight yourself.
Even when you do it every day. We knew
we were going to crack. We knew it would
happen. We tried to do all the right
things. Tried to adapt. But even though
we are hip to all the traps, all the
coverups, all the lies we invent to fool
ourselves, and all the other lies on sale,
the soldier still sits there.

Some of those old aphorisms are right,
maybe. But if old soldiers fade away,
which is rather a nice image, and young
soldiers fall down go boom or blow up
or some other equally dramatic or uninspired
manner, how about old soldiers never die,
we wish they would all just go away. See,
soldier is a metaphor here. You know,
for all of us who've been conscripted,
screwed and thrown away. Dig?

I THOUGHT SOME MORE.

It is intellectually possible to know
that being a soldier, a fighting soldier,
is an odd, a weird, and probably a wrong
job, but there is something about it,
if you did it right, something so translucent
and so thick, a feeling so old and fresh
(why do fools fall in love) it cannot
leave or be thrown out. Oh, we try to
shed that skin, but we keep it in the
closet. And try it on now and then.
And even if it does not fit, it does.
Ask yourself if you feel as old as you
are. I know a man with no legs who
doesn't know it.

TOMBSTONE.

We don't want to get too much meaning
out of this.

83.

I came to a surrealization.

TOMBSTONE, TO THE WIDOW.

You here for a good time, or do you
have a bag of wrath?

LIGHTS WENT OFF, LEFT A GLOW.

Could see her a mile off,
a thought clad in rags.

84.

Woke up with blood on my face, an old wound festered in a dream, was I shot while dreaming?

TOMBSTONE.

Dead warrior. A rested fury. Arrested fury.

TOMBSTONE.

The man who came to an unsatisfactory conclusion.

TOMBSTONE.

So many died for that short life.

85.

Very strong guns, their range is forever.
Fuck muzzle velocity. The bullets that
hit me are heading for someone else
right now, twenty years later.

86.

Ever been shot in the face before?
Ever shoot anybody in the face before?
What does being a warrior mean?

I SPAT STRAIGHT AHEAD.

It clung to the leaf. I looked at that
piece of myself. Hanging, bobbing by
its own weight, waiting until it fell.
A mountain climber in a silent fall.

TOMBSTONE.

They were boys then. Does the extra
"dead time" make them men now?

WATER DOESN'T RHYME WITH LATER.

Our sleek heads trying to repel the
sound of rain. Fuck the wet. It
was the noise that killed you. I'll
contradict that later.

87.

Ever feel tampered with?

INSIDE THE EARTH.

Felt like the earth was trembling, it
was shaking.

TOMBSTONE.

My own heart sent me flowers. The rose
is in the air, the rose understands.

THE RAIN.

Somehow, it seemed that rain was what
was coming down after the sun blew up.

88.

Confused, miserable, and wet. Sort
of like a dizzy rat in a funhouse.

CLEAN PLACE, CLEAN DAY.

Do they rake this woods? What a little
day. Such a small day.

89.

The frost of apprehension. Appeal on his face. Upheaval on his face.

TOMBSTONE.

I'm becoming inattentive. The weather really came at us.

90.

Father, how does it feel to be dead? Can you hear me? What's it like, watching me, not being able to warn me?

TOMBSTONE.

Nice to see you, general.

OLD LIGHTNING.

We found a couple blades over by the trees.
I never really believed it at first, that
it really goes for trees, it did not
make any sense. But when you get close
up, I mean right up to them, you can see
the guilt. They try to turn away. I
don't know what they're trying to hide.
But, why would lightning just fling itself
down into forests like that. Aiming at
the tallest trees. I would sort of
like a regiment of lightning of my own.
You know, train it, let it loose, see
what happens. We could have used it
over there. We did to some extent, secretly.
But the blades I found were still in
pretty good shape. The color was a bit
weak, the edge a little dull. But it
moved when it saw us. Kind of scared at
first. It snapped and hissed, and
tried to roll over and get up. That
stuff's pretty wild. But once you get it
in the bag, you know, where it's dark.
It settles down. Might even sleep in there.
That's when to feed it. When it's out
cold. It ain't dumb. It knows where the
food came from.

SETTLE ON IT.

Whine, or zip, or hum, or something.
Writers always settle for a word
for the sound that bullets make when
they go right by your head. Like Eskimos
have how many, a million words for snow?
Like what it looks like in the sun, and
so on. That's interesting. Well, there
are many sounds that bullets make.
The sound (oh yes, let's not forget whistling,
re: first line) that bullets make right
by your ear, six feet away, a hundred
meters. There is also a sound a slug
makes when it hits. The big question is
what makes the sound. The slug or the
flesh it hits. If you could slow it
way down, we could imagine many sounds
for the flesh flying out in little clumps,
or splatters, or even in huge hunks.
Like a handful, an armload, a mouthful,
that was a mouthful, that was an eyeful.
Sometimes, depending on the size of the
slug, an entire person can be gone and
you cannot remember any sound at all.
The person is gone, but something in that
nothingness remains. Perhaps just a little
sound, if I may be allowed to contradict
myself. For a change.

91.

Two cats on fire bolted straight up
a palm and were gone as they left reality.

92.

This one is true. One of the guys in
my squad was a black man from Missouri.
A farmer with a wife. He looked a lot
like my father. He dropped a sniper
and was so goddamn happy. That really
impressed me too.

TOMBSTONE.

Jesus, I'm tired. I mean I'm really beat.

TOMBSTONE.

A certain element of discontent is necessary
to spur men on to a higher life. Did
I write that?

93.

Attempted murder does a lot to clear the air.

94.

Beans of light.

95.

A new truth must be provided.

IT WAS A MURDEROUS MOSAIC.

Heightened somewhat by one thousand hits of acid and the Bible.

TOMBSTONE.

If we had been quicker, we'd have been
in the valley or ravine in no time.

96.

There must be a crowd in my head.

BATTLEGROUND.

Thunderplace.

TOMBSTONE.

Just the other night I was everywhere at once.

97.

Black wind, darkness. Does it come off?

98.

Holding a big chunk of red.

99.

Winds through the trees were screaming as from compulsive helium use.

100.

Find yourself   quick.

DO YOU EVER.

Feel small and grey with a light grey background, or not?

101.

That country is a very large reliquary.

TOMBSTONE.

Screwed in my soul, snowed in my soul.

TOMBSTONE.

I have learned to, when I'm angry and sad to snort in my breath and suck in my heart. Did that all fit?

102.

I learned to compensate in the most obvious ways.

SO I WAS WONDERING.

Do the Chinese use lunchmeat for lilypads, sometimes?

INTERPRET THIS.

Everybody's made of leather.

TOMBSTONE.

Looking up at the rotten clouds.

THE VOICE RISES ON THIS ONE.

War is on that hill, war is over there
war is waiting in the morning. There is
war in my fuckin' head. It's in my
clothes, in my walk, in my stare, in my
style. It's in my fuckin' clothes
for Christ's sake. You think it's only in
the book, only in the dreams?

103.

When we were there we sometimes lost our heads. Now that some of us are back we have had to undergo a sort of recapitation.

TOMBSTONE.

A poem which is a story about a war that will not end. What, the poem or the war?

YOU ARE NOT WITHOUT FRIENDS.

You're not without wicked and dangerous friends.

104.

The contradiction business.

IT.

Made me what I always wanted to be, made me do things I never could do, made me do things I would never do.

TOMBSTONE.

I am among you.

SORT OF HOW I FEEL.

Don't touch me (yet) I'm baffled.
I'm not ready yet.

105.
ROUND.

The rich and evil made fools of us then.
We should let them know we're on to them now.

106.

We were bullies from outer space.

I THOUGHT.

Life could go on without me. A very pale very misty thought. Sing a long verse. Stop abruptly. Let the band carry on for a while.

TOMBSTONE.

A personal tragedy struck.

WHAT?

Life is many things to some people. No, life is many things to one person. No, life is one thing to many people. No, wait, to many people, life is really something. Like life, one thing to many people, is something.

107.

When she screamed, ancient fire trucks came storming out of her mouth.

TOMBSTONE.

A life that had been all dirtied up by meaning.

POINT MAN.

The guy was a goner, grip free, out
to several meals. A real case on point.

Highland red.

The dirt is dry and red. A fella could
do sand paintings out here. Only thing
is nobody could tell what you did, red
on red. A red Reinhardt.

LAST MOVE.

Some people were found with their hands
locked in a death grip, buried deep into
the roots of their hair. Dead from
exasperation and helplessness. Trying
to pull the hair out in an immature show
of frustration.

108.

It seems rather ironic that we're being paid to do this.

HOT.

It's so goddamn hot. Wouldn't it be funny to just switch off the light, be dark just like that. Nobody'd know except us. That would fool 'em.

109.

Spare parts, we could build the most interesting people from them.

110.

Good God man, are you mad?

111.

Made an idea smile like a lantern.

112.

A clever little path leading us on.

113.

Stronghold or weakhold.

114.

Some of the parallels are so parallel.

AN OLD CUSTOM.

Shaking the overhead leaves after a heavy rain, the rain was hot and stinking. It was a "piñata of piss".

115.

A hard, shiny green. Leaves like large beetle shells.

116.

Soft colors.

TOMBSTONE.

Oh save your breath.

TOMBSTONE.

Primordial
meditative
objective

MARKER.

On places where people had died a little burned patch appeared. Even rocks were scorched, and rivers hissed with steam.

CURLED.

Held his rifle in his arms like a little teddy and died. An odd little comfort, indeed.

117.

A redundancy I could live with. Shrank into a million pieces.

118.

A lizard ran up the wall of trees. A cheap outdoor hotel.

TOMBSTONE.

It was the perfect cliche, no one would ever believe it.

TOMBSTONE.

The sound of roses in the night.

119.

Weasling around this jungle abbey
rattling vines.

120.

God, we're sharp and just as dull.
The razor's edge of stupidity.

PART ONE.

A person's need for solitude, his need to kill, the kinship of man and plant, the flesh of the tree, the bark of man.

PART TWO.

The place was made of everything. You'd sink in it, you'd break on it, you'd bounce off things, you would absorb each other, and then simultaneously reject. Eating and vomiting at the same time.

PART THREE.

Tried to shake the doubt.

121.

OK, now remind me of something else, different.

122.

I went out and had some (an) illusions. Honey, that's no lie.

TOMBSTONE.

A pleasant surprise is in store for you.

123.

We tried all that time to stay alive, sort of. Now that we're all safe, we try to kill ourselves.

TOMBSTONE.

Oh me, no more me.

VARY.

It wasn't so easy long ago. You couldn't
always pick your own time.
It wasn't so easy long ago. You couldn't
pick your time, always.

124.

I find nothing beautiful in love or the act of love.

APHORISM.

Went some place we'd never been. Now we're all from there.

125.

Rained drops of blood. A bad storm.
Golfball size balls of flesh.

THE WHISPERERS.

Go home
you are home

stay here
stay here forever

with us.

126.

Anxiety was about waist high.

127.

The air smelled strongly of witches.

TOMBSTONE.

An obvious past, pocked with indecision.

128.

Let's wait, the hesitants concurred.

TOMBSTONE.

We can't take it back
we can't give it back.

TOMBSTONE.

He looked heavily around him.

TOMBSTONE.

Paper boys paper man.

PART OF A POEM.

heard the cussing of the wind.

EVERYTHING IS ANSWERABLE.

You fascinate me. Shut up.

TOMBSTONE.

He always had that look on his face
that sunshine causes.

TOMBSTONE.

Did it start there or end there?

TOMBSTONE.

I'm not very bright in the morning.

BELIEF.

I can go back, I know I can...

TOMBSTONE.

Sing about the bad times.

SOLVE THIS.

Present calamity, this trend of death.

AFTERFIGHT.

Scars on the air like deep scratches
made with an auger or bottle opener.

YOU CAN WALK AROUND IT LIKE A LASER PICTURE.

Or as if they were frozen like the screams,
waiting.

FIRST.

Bells were placed in every tree that remained. If the tree was too young a gong was tied to it.

SECOND.

Guys with hoods like monks from all over the world, all religions, even not religions, bogus monks there for effect. Really beautifully dressed, like some minor popes.

TOMBSTONE.

A stormy finish.

THIRD.

There was a tense silence like just before lightning decides who to hit and who to miss.

129.

When I rose, I was a bullet.
Twenty bullets. All with one mind.
Find it and alter it.

130.

Some kind of ray.

COME ON.

Come on, die like me. Open your mouth,
stick out your tongue, catch a bullet
in your lips. You can do it if you try.
Come on, die like me.

TOMBSTONE.

and the moonlight's yellow.
and the river's bitter.

TOMBSTONE.

Don't look me in the eye, read my lips.

RECOVERY.

I felt as if all my prehensile limbs
had been ripped off. Torn off.
Like straining for a glass of beer
with my stump.

131.

Freud said we never forget anything.
Well fuck'im. I saw him without his
bowtie once.

OFF TO MY RIGHT.

A little puddle of a helmet full of brains
an after of afterthought.

TOMBSTONE.

Her name escapes me now. I chase though.

WHEN.

When he blew up, his teeth, dog tags and
beads flew out into space like the tracers
aimed at ships in Victory at Sea.
Shining, off target, until lost in the
dark of space, unrecoverable.

TINY PRAYER.

Give my heart some light.
Carve me up inside.
Heart looked like an ice sculpture
of an old shell.

132.

Walked so much, we should be in Africa by
now.

TOMBSTONE.

Fear. Dig it out with a spoon.
Dig a hole with a knife.

TOMBSTONE.

What is the conclusion?

NICE IDEA.

The violins in the trees, thirty feet up.

133.

The guy was happy to be gut-shot.

WISH.

If you could only put your feet up when you walk.

WISH TWO.

Horses really would have made this tough going, remember Sergeant?

I IMAGINE A FINE THING.

You shout so loud so long your voice
finally shreds like fine, long fringe
until it is only a whispering waving
battle flag fluttering from your cavelike
mouth.

SOME THOUGHT ON DEATH.

Death is important. It assumes a greater role the nearer it is, the longer it tends to endure. It lasts longer than many things. I suppose some rivers are as old as many deaths.

TOMBSTONE.

Standing there like morons.

KILLED SINGERS.

Nobody can hear you now, everybody really
cares, but they are bloody mutes too.
If all the noise but the voices was taken
away, you would hear hundreds of snakes.
All men. Horse is the wrong animal here.
I think this is a reference to Picasso's
famous painting. Many fine tenors were
lost here. Let us not forget the castrati nouveau
with no guaranteed careers.

FACES IN THE TREES.

Look closely at the trees. See faces?
Sure you do. See, there's Bela Lugosi,
my favorite. And other twisted saints.
You just see who you know. Usually.
Way better than clouds.

134.

Moronic fucking trees.

WHY.

Why does something that lasts only two weeks or two months or two years become so important for so long after so long? An instant of trauma can cause trauma that lasts forever, and not just your forever.

THIS.

Clearing was made by an air-burst at tree-top level. A whole big area cleared. Trees stripped like hundreds of crazy lawn mowers on their own. Even the blown down parts, clean. Like it was made by a strange magic trick gone bad. All that was needed was some swirling green clouds, or maybe colored fuzz blowing around.

135.

Even in my dreams I feign sleep and dreaming.

BREAKFAST.

Or a box or bowl of Instant Death.

HOW'D THEY KNOW?

Walking along we'd see our own names carved on trees. First, last, and middle initial in some cases. Boy, they knew a lot. Kind of a funny feeling.

REALLY PREENED.

The hills had been perfectly prepared. It was obvious thousands of French maids had been hired to clean and sweep the forests and hillsides. Rocks were finely polished, trees buffed. All the leaves were washed or recently sprayed and touched up with the proper color. Everything was perfect.

136.

Birds flew over to reassure us.

137.

Colors, glowing clouds, you could tell
something was going to happen.

MOTHS.

Moths came at us by the millions. They
made a low thumping sound when they hit
hard, and kind of a leathery casual slippery
hush when they brush by you in flight.
Almost like the sound made when you shine
the toes of your shoes on the backs of
your trouser legs. Or the low bubbling
of an old man bringing up phlegm when you have
a pretty bad cold, or he is dying. The
aftersound is tremendous. After they've
glanced off you enough, for hours, they
thunder into the trees leaving slight
gashes on themselves and the soft-barked
trees. The residue of powder is immense.
You must wade through it thick as powdered
sugar. It reflects the sun like crazy.
And can put your eye out.

REVERSAL.

Addled by truth, less and less by lies.

TOMBSTONE.

An undeniable history, a reproachable history.

138.

Livin' in this tree is a scary thing.
I'm so high up.

139.

It is so easy to hate, it is so hard to hate. Must be going now, it's getting late.

140.

Powdered by the sun, whipped by the wind.

YOU MEET ALL KINDS.

One of the privates in the company, who, it seemed to me, was a loner, even though he was constantly talking, had a severe problem with his nose. He was always blowing it or dabbing it. You could hear him over every other sound except for that one sound. He sat too near me one day. But even under the circumstances, it would have been rude to move. I mean, how obvious can you get? He was snorting and carrying on with his nose like it was a precision instrument that he got for free. He was twisting it, bending it, rubbing it, even pounding on it from the top. He took out his handkerchief, a twisted clot of god knows what and blew with most of his might. I presume he conserved enough air for two more expulsions. To my horror, and his delight, and chimp-like fascination, a wad of ants flew out and kept on coming. His nose had become a repository for the beasts overnight. And there was no hiding his glee. A fellow down the line remarked, "Now whomever shall write his letters?"

FIVE PART PIECE.

1.
Here are the bags full of night you
ordered. Here are the baskets of shadows.
Here, too, the jars of grim thought.

2.
Tried to shake, shook the doubt.

3.
I'm like a fire in what ways I don't know.

4.
I heard a faint sound. I took it to be a
laugh from my groin area.

5.
The air was full of bullets. How much
air do you think was displaced?

SIXTEEN TOMBSTONES IN A ROW.

TOMBSTONE.
1.
Their love was deeper than ours.
TOMBSTONE.
2.
When will the spring come?
TOMBSTONE.
3.
I may not always be right, but it looks
that way. But I have to seem like I'm right.
TOMBSTONE.
4.
I live because I made it so.
TOMBSTONE.
5.
I am my own fantasy.
TOMBSTONE.
6.
I wish I was something else.
TOMBSTONE.
7.
They went where they shouldn't.
TOMBSTONE.
8.
Looking through ice.

TOMBSTONE.
9.
Real bad
Way too bad.
TOMBSTONE.
10.
Got a runaway mind
and a runaway guilt
two things on which
the world was built.
TOMBSTONE.
11.
I understand everything now, of course.
Life and death, the important stuff.
How we breathe and how we grow
how we suck and how we know.
TOMBSTONE.
12.
Send me a sum commensurate with your guilt.
TOMBSTONE.
13.
The sense of drama.
TOMBSTONE.
14.
She wanted to be remembered.
TOMBSTONE.
15.
I'm tired. Keep up.
TOMBSTONE.
16.
A personal fascination of mine is the unmet.

I'VE BEEN A RAT.

Even I know that. I don't think I tried
to be. Some things just work that way.
Yes, I've been a rat, but I took the bait.
Just goin' around wreckin' shit.

CONFIRMATION.

My mother will confirm this:
I had to be a man by myself.
"Yes, son, you said that."
See?

TOMBSTONE.

I can't go this far. And I can't go no
farther.

SNAKES.

Snakes, they're everything shitty anyone
has ever said about them. They <u>are</u> cold.
They <u>are</u> mean. They <u>are</u> slimey. They
<u>can</u> smell fear. Every guy I ever knew who
got bit was scared. They hang in trees
like shitty little banners waiting for
a parade. Then they jump or swing or
otherwise insinuate down upon the previously
snake-free person.
They are a lot like dentists. They smile
and stick you. They like their work.
There is a sense of accomplishment.
Pain and death. Sometimes the "others"
would hide snakes in tunnels. A living
booby trap. We'd come down the hole and
WAP. A snakebite in the lips. Count to
three and it's goodbye Jim. Did we ever
use snakes for traps? Fuck no. First
of all, we wouldn't touch the miserable little
creeps, and next, the "others" weren't
afraid of snakes. Christ, they'd <u>eat</u> snakes.
They lived with the fuckers. I think they
were part snake. Livin' in holes, hiding
in trees, lookin' like sticks, bein'
quiet, slinkin' 'roun' bein' sinister
and plannin' shit on us in the dark,
when it rains, only when its shitty
out.

2 ANIMALS.

The time 2 animals came straight at ME. Not caring a BIT if I was a huge SPIDER web or a big wet LAKE. I knew CHOICES needed to be made. So I made some. The first seems extravagant NOW, though I must admit it caused a certain furor in the climes wherein I was residing. WILDLY. I needn't tell you what they were.

TOMBSTONE.

There was the fleeting expression,
frozen on his face forever.

TOMBSTONE.

How soon will it be 'til the politicians
will lay down with the snakes?

141.

It is too bad about some guys. One who shouldn't have been shot was a silly likeable fat person.

142.

I hope some of them think about this stuff. After all, they were the bad guys.

143.

When you're on patrol, you can think of the strangest things. Like what is the Pope's favorite lotion.

144.

I don't want to tell you everything. I'm afraid I'll run out of things to say.

TOMBSTONE.

If I wake up from this, I'll never.........
I promise.

145.

It's funny that with so much to say, we continue to wallow around in secrecy.

146.

I wrote to a dead friend's girlfriend. The handwriting burned into the table beneath the paper.

THEM.

The air was charged with malignancy. So were their bunkers.

SICK.

After those world class hangovers, I would sometimes be observed trying to bite the sunlight on the floor. Trying to scratch the light sun on the floor?

WET COMPARISON.

After the rain, I saw the company dullard.
His folded arms opening just so. Like
a wet butterfly. He was oblivious.
A slow, wet fluttttttter. A nervous twitch
with wings.

CRASH.

A butterfly came straight at me and
crashed into my head. Neither one of us
fell down.

147.

I found his arrogance, his condescending attitude, his slovenly flatulent appearance insulting and disgusting. He made a lovely target.

148.

You don't necessarily have to look great.
Just make sure you want to look the
way you look. Look the way you want to
look.

149.

This is something that is impossible to get rid of, like wiping the bugs off the inside of the windshield.

AFTERNOON DISCUSSION.

Sometimes, to spend the time, we would sit around and tell lies. This, I am sure, continues to this day. One of the guys noted that the smell of a gunfight was remotely like that of creamed corn. He was properly admonished. Somebody threw a helmet of piss at him.

150.

When you're in the same movie three or more times, it starts to get predictable.

REMARKABLE.

Some of the whores were mystical. Well-read. Experts in the humanities. One slight bright yellow girl looked like she stepped out of a Chagall. Smiling, a fiddle in her fist, (rather obvious, she admitted later) she told me of her devotion to dance and Chagall's early interest in the ballet. She speculated on her own place in world history.

FINALLY.

Finally, back home, I fall in love.
She was skinny and tentative. She was gorgeous, in other words.

VIEW.

Many of them couldn't see what was happening. They were blind inside. When you are sitting on a nameless mountain with nowhere to go but down, your levels of awareness are sometimes limited to thirst, hunger and a hole.

I KNOW THE HORROR.

We could tell he was wounded. The trail he left was a mark of his youth. Plants flattened, little gasps of terror hanging from branches. Sometimes unflattering animal imagery is best. He panicked like a semi-wild hog.

MELANCHOLY.

Sometimes, overcome with memory, covered with soiled mail, rolling in a pile of medals, I start dancing. Hard, like a pig.

YOU REMIND ME OF A MUSEUM.

Finally, through an inarticulate proposal and walking into the subdawn, I smelled through your veil the increased irony. Don't confuse panic with love.

151.

I want to do a painting of you. And in it, I want to use some symbolic stuff about time.

EYE ON YOURSELF.

Seeing yourself slowly going insane. Maintaining a big manly laugh.

YOUR WAR.

So, while I was over in Indochina, living a colorful existence, you were "being interesting" and taking grey people as lovers.

152.

The new knowledge was hot. All in vain. The knowledge was not all in vain.

153.

All wet and disheveled, all wet and disinherited.

BAGGED ALIVE.

It's hot under here, and it's hard to breathe. I trust you can hear me clearly, for I am nearly done.

154.

War souvenir. I can't take care o' no lizard.

TOMBSTONE.

Get outa my light.

ROUGH EPITAPH.

I have seen my own shadow, and I don't like it.

FOREST NOISES.

Precious songs, priceless.

155.

The body count, used here as a pronoun, lay fallow. Fat and yellow.

ACCEPTABLE BEHAVIOR.

Let me act like a baby wonce.

HANGING.

The smoke hung around after the fight
like draperies. Dirty, bloody ones.
It woulda been good to have been able to
pull them shut. But, as everyone knows,
smoke is hard to control.

RIDING DOWN THE ROAD.

Old crones offered their jewelry; black
smiles.

FLIES.

Wish you'd a been born a horse, or had
a tail or you were issued a tail. Umm,
tail, just a piece of tail.

DEAR JOHN.

I do not think "Dear John" is the proper term for that type of letter. Why not think of some other possibilities?
Dear Fool
Dear Jerk
Dear Poor Fucker
You might not like what I'm about to say.
You'll always have a place in my heart and my memory.
Well, thanks, you'll always have a place in my sights, and my memory.

156.

Ironically, I loved getting mail from the lying bastards at home.

WORK.

No matter what you do for a living, some of us didn't even do anything for a living, yet...
Some of us still don't do anything for a living. But there we were, (you finish the line.) Except for yardwork, and busboy, this was our first job. It has really done us a lot of good so far. The army work experience. I have actually put down KILLER on job applications in the "previous positions held" blank. Do you know that not even the army will have us now?

A BEATING.

I recall them taking my conscience into the shed where they worked it over with groundskeeping equipment.

LIKENESS.

We were all sharp and lean, like we'd
never been fed, never.
Alert as if our mothers had been cats,
our fathers educated sprinters.

WISH.

I wished that Franz Marc could have been in my outfit to paint out some of the young or all of the bad.

SITTING.

Sitting around like lug-nuts. Sometimes you look behind you and see the most frightening things.

REMARKABLE.

He had the art of lightning in him.

FROM THE NOTEBOOK.

A dragonfly has six legs, four wings,
two on each side of its body. Two high
and low. The body, the abdomen has six
sections and a butt. There are two
large eyes and has no ungainly antennae.
To bend and break and compromise its view
or impair its senses, that is.

A HEARTFELT WHEW.

Getting out of here reasonably alive
seems to be to our advantage.

BUT THAT'S O.K.

This is the story, this is the deal.
As we grow older, we realize that
we've been grazed by sentimentality.

CLEAR MORNING.

I got into a river once. It seemed very long. I could see both ways for a long way. The water was cold. Like our mountain rivers. Clear and shallow with small smooth stones on the bed and large sharp rocks on the shore. There was heavy brush about five feet off the shore.
I got in and my dink shrunk to nothing.
Just as well, I was not going trolling.
So we filled the river with soap, and probably gave away our position. It was pretty though.

QUICK QUESTION.

Would it be alright to say that some of us were on edge?

PART OF THE JOB.

Some of them suffered from varying degrees of officerness.

SITTING AROUND.

Never bored, always something to do,
or something to hate. You could always
sit around and hate something...

DISABLED.

I still wake up with the sound of nighthawks in my ears.

NEW WAR.

If they did something we had never heard of, could it be considered esoteric warfare?

SURPRISE.

The first time I loaded my rifle,
I was surprised to note that the
bullets came from the same arsenal
that my mother worked for in WW II.
Strange. I have nothing more to add
to that.

DESIRE.

I want to take up with those Chinese
geese. I want to be migrating
up and migrate out. Take up with those
geese. Maybe end up in Canada.

TOMBSTONE.

It's natural causes. I won't be dead
very long.

NOT MUCH INTEREST.

I really don't give much of a shit about
space travel.

ALL I NEED.

Somebody came to my home at one a.m. and rang the doorbell. I got up to answer it. There was no visible person there. I walked out, on to the sidewalk, leaving the doors wide open, inner and outer. I came back in and checked the rear door and stepped on a piece of glass. Now I smell someone near me. The doors are closed. We are in for the night.

157.

Gun positions were sitting high, placed quickly, set up with reasonable care. Sort of like shrines, I think. Regarded with certain reverence by the unbelievers.

BARRICADES.

Things will crop up to prevent you from leaving. But from that you will learn.

THE BLUE FLOWER.

There should have been a flower. I wish there had been a blue flower. Not so much a field of them, just one. A small flower with short wide petals. With a little yellow center. A little of that pollen business dusted on the base of the petals. But here's the high light. When you look at the flower, from a distance, it really sticks out. When you look closely, you can see the sky in there. You know, light blue, high blue sometimes, with those filmy white clouds moving clockwise, from petal to petal, then the random storm, like in real life.

STRANGE CONSTRAINT.

How does a prince or baron or whatever
the hell I am hold on to my riches when
there is so much change going on around
me? Whereas, art is so passionate that
it sustains you. It was so early, you
could cut it with a knife. In order
to keep track of time, I have a beautiful
woman hand me a flower one minute before
each hour begins. Something inside wants
you to stay up so you won't miss it.
Kisses close in like gunshots. Then I
loved her. She went by and my ears started
ringing. She created an atmosphere.
I think I heard smiling in the bush.
Details blend into a larger thing. For
a short time I felt that we were kings
picnicking in the mountains. Ring those
bells. I got to talk to someone I love.
I was rather amusing don't you,...you are
not solidified. Alright, I will evaporate
then. A hole in the horrid blue sky.
Delay, no reaction. It took a year before
I heard the scream. Shadow passed over
me like a snake. I became a real viet-man.
Sitting there waiting for each other to
die. I miss all the music of not making love.

SNIPERS.

Seeing artistically should be like fighting dirty. Use all your means. Look around things, look through things, look until a thing stays seen. Use your head. Scratch and claw with all your senses. Don't worry about what you cannot control. Remember to be amused by your own attitudes. At times. (I've seen all the pictures. He stopped looking.) You are in a new environment. Your eyes tell you that I want you to think. Maybe you're not interested, you can't love everything. But you can think it over. Just remember to keep your eyes in the trees.

THINGS LOOKED PRETTY ROUGH.

We came onto the battlesite one day late.
We could tell there had been a lot of
noise. There were implied screams all
over the place. Busted necks, blood on
the branches. Tons of feathers remained
all over the place. Especially the
white ones. They were not the big white
ones, not like the good ones for hats.
Short, unimpressive feathers from short dead
birds. Down floated around. Who would
rip off their chests? Legs were strung
from the lower limbs. It may have been,
but did not look like a silent demise.
This place looks kind of holy. All
the silver smoke, the smiley skulls, the
shiny wet rocks and shreds of sturdy
cloth. This place looks kinda holy.
The water runs through, glittering
like a ditch full of diamonds. Pretty
holy alright. There are plenty of little
dents in the dirt, made no doubt, by
the knees of praying losers.

OCTOBER 16.

Making himself invisible. Put on camouflage, tape dog tags, blousing rubbers on pants. Clean ammo, sharpen knife, check springs. Straighten pins on grenades. No metal on metal. Hard gear behind. Soft gear up front. Tiger claw always worn toward your heart. There is something special. Fantastic. Grown up, sophisticated, about owning your own life. A big green mess, the smells limped along the jungle floor, leaving a weak trail. Wonderful monsters, gave me the great creeps. I am often in the fifty-second state. A state of mind characterized by a free uncorrupted mentality. Sometimes, simply for the fun of it, I creep through the weeds until I come upon a tree only feet away. Its own rustling covers my rustlings. In this way, I observe its alertness. Which is usually poor. Trees are often unaware of danger. Compared to other things.

Be on edge, reluctant sunset. It is the
color we chose. Do not yawn, a secret
may fly out. I am riding an alligator,
I am too far gone to not become a bird.
A lot of us were just too civilized to have
killed so many people. But they could
not jump through my eyes and fool us or
swim in my head. Whatever, and what have
you, and this type of thing. A highlight
like that can take a lot of the suspense
out of the day. A guy ran, a guy almost
fell down, almost died. I killed him.
I killed him hard. So little accomplished
for so much work. I wonder if anybody thinks
of or remembers me. Do you? There is music.
I am alive now. The imperfect dignity.
Let time pass. One day goes, comes another.
Become visible.

THE GRAVE ROBBER.

Old, rundown and somber. Under water, sucking on a hope reed. A mental hobo. A twisted heart, a busted mind, a little grace. What, is this stuff gonna break my heart or something? Killin' ain't so tough, it's livin' with it. The big challenge here is being able to put up with all this work and live together without choking each other. We all cope with varying degrees of success. Yes, I know I am heavily dependent on the same air every one else breathes. My heart says I'm right. The only person you're screwing is yourself. You reap what you fuckin' sow. The whole idea of art is substituting one thing for another... cool, yet perplexing. Sounded like the passing of civilization. So, some of us exploded in different amounts. Some in pieces of legs, pieces of arms, some into pieces of mind. Some were found in the fecal position. I saw the birds so pissed they balled their little feet into little fists. They want the whole woods. Who does? The little animals in the woods. The trees looked like mules had been eating on them. Nice work all of you, and especially some of you.

ONE MORNING.

Rabbits in the house, half were feeding
on speed, the others sedated for the
contrast of big hares padding around
and the leaping, flying around ones
glancing off bookshelves and breaking china.

TOMBSTONE.

Had my country pulled out from underneath me.

TOMBSTONE.

The cold glitters.

TOMBSTONE.

On those autumn days.

TOMBSTONE.

I will still protect her from monsters.

IT WAS THE MORNING.

It was the morning I found the cow's
head. The little red lizards were all
over the place, jumping around like
grasshoppers on a hot day. Some could
get as high as my belt if they got a run.
It <u>was</u> a hot day. A brief wind came in
on its knuckles, and made some rough
noises. This brought some leaves down
from the lower trees which blew into
the stream. That's where the head was.
Kind of smiling with one eye open.
Alright, it's been unleashed. Life,
yes, it was eludesome. I have been
sifting through my wreckage. We were
victims of a dark scheme. I felt dumb.
I sighed like the dog I hit when I first
got my driver's permit. My hair was clubbing
me to death. Little known things, forgotten
facts, things often not mentioned. Warnings.
The small things, like how do you feel.
Evasive things, things held back, things
to look out for. Walking through bullshit.
That thing that is gone is really here to
stay. This is, of course, a grey area.
Let's rewind the night. No thank you.
I will just sit here in the dusk and stifle
my cough.

BEFORE CHRISTMAS.

I had asked her to send me something
special from home. I keenly wanted
Hubert Humphrey to send a state flag.
I opened the package, beaten up like
an old drunk. I savored the postmark;
Glen Lake, Minnesota. I opened it up.
Homemade cookies, the best in the world.
Liberal magazines. Socks, soft drink
powders. I read the letters. Then read
them again. Something was going on behind
me. A few strident calls, familiar, out
of place. Flashes of blue, then white.
A burst of yellow. Three bluejays and a
goldfinch had stowed away, for me. For
my mind and my soul. And over there, on
a cattail, deep in the green black wet
tropical jungle, one of the most beautiful
red-wing blackbirds.

MOTTO.

I much prefer dark and solitude to light
and people.

IN THE CHOPPER. I'M A COLONEL.

I saw them fall, I saw them die. I saw
chunks of land explode and change shape
and size. It was a strange quilt lying
on the slope. Different than the quilt
I have at home which reminds me of apple
trees, fishing and cows, rather than
the quilt I now see made of shredded
earth and men, in the three colors of
war: green, brown and red. Depending
on the quilt.

TOMBSTONE.

OK, now one of you with a pocket calculator
figure this out; Multiply the 21 bullets
you just fired for my "salute" by the number
of good guys killed, add the number of
bad guys killed, and ALL the civilians killed.
Count one half for the wounded in all categories.
Ask the French if they want in. Sure, call
China. Take the war related suicides and
bereaved heart attack victims and the
certifiably mad, make an effigy for each
one out of cheese and shit, and have a
display on the white house lawn. Or would
that be too much trouble? Hey, I'm joking.
I'm dead. Besides, nothing's carved in stone.

IF I COULD ONLY BELIEVE YOU.

There is something about this scene, something false, man made or tampered with. I know the villagers are dead. I know that. But more than that. It is more lifeless than that. Like life has been starched. The death too. Like the shooting stopped instantly. The wounded froze into death and the smoke went rigid in its ascent. Clouds don't move. Here. If I didn't know better, I'd think that Van Gogh and Goya came in here with a few tons of paint and spent a week or two. There was a messy little trail of paint and some very noticeable spit. I took that for Vincent's. No doubt they were looking for a jungle bistro. A loose pile of wine bottles strewn about. Some chicken bones, and of all things, some ladies' clothing and some soiled paint rags.

Makes one wonder what the hell goes on
in this world. There were some notes
in Spanish written on stiff paper, and
then more wine bottles leading me on.
Another mile or so into a clearing.
There the bastards were. Both of them.
Drunker than shit. Bullfighting with a
couple of the local water buffalo. The
few spectators were going wild, screaming
in a peculiar blend of Spanish and Vietnamese
calling for blood no doubt. Francisco
was the more energetic of the two, and
he had a palette knife in his teeth and
a very long bamboo pole with a good stiff
brush affixed to its end. There was red
on it. Paint, I assume. The buffalo
would make its pass and Goya would plant
a crimson cross wherever he could. He
was pretty drunk and the crosses were
fairly bold and sloppy.

Vincent did his best to distract the
buffalo when Francisco took a drink.
The fans were going nuts. They were slugging
Thai Whiskey as fast as they could find
their mouths. Vincent, I noticed, would
be smoking marijuana in a long white
pipe, then pass it along to one of his
pals who would smile broadly and nod
his head. Christ, this was much better
than a cockfight. Two famous European
artists having the time of their lives
in Kontum Province. One of the buffalo,
either jealous or bored, came at Francisco
from behind. Vincent shouted in slurred
French and let fly two wine bottles. He
must have aimed, because they both hit
the left eye and drew him off for a second.
Francisco sidestepped. Light on his
feet as the ballerinas he loved, he stuck
his knife deep into the buffalo's throbbing
vein. This is not what I wanted, he yelled
across the field of glory. Let's take
off. I am yours with a handshake, replied
Vincent, and they shot off into the grove,
leaving their paint, but carting the wine
in a lovely canvas bag. Their signatures
fell lightly to the ground as they
disappeared into the wet green history.

LIFE WAS, DEATH IS.

A brief flirtation with existentialism.
Listen to the rodents bearing news. The
sound so loud you can't hear screaming.
I'd call that an extreme of some sort.
There is not truth in beauty, no beauty
in truth. It does not exist. Only the
lie persists. All too frequently, you
overestimate your personal powers. I'm
out gathering nicknames. He assumed
power. As if he personally, and deliberately
had and (quite unofficially) endowed
the object with magical powers. A good
day for a hangin', a fine day for bein'
almost human. Slept in a slit, and sat
backwards in a pool of tears. That's
something that occurs only, oh, every
once, every, um, ten or twelve years.
In the dead sand. A minute or two. He
did not expect to be here long. A
slender bend of brightness. I never
went outside. There isn't much of a day
left considering what is up on that hill.
Distant thump. Sounded like they were
dancing in wooden boots, trousers, and
hats made of fire.

DISTANT THUMP.

Sounded like we were dancing in wooden
boots, trousers, and hats made of fire.
There isn't much of a day left considering
what is up on that hill. A slender bend of
brightness. I never went outside.
In the dead sand, a minute or two, he
did not expect to be here long. That's
something that occurs only, oh, every
once, every, um, ten or twelve years.
Slept in a slit, and sat backwards in a
pool of tears. A good day for a hangin',
a fine day for bein' almost human. He
assumed power. As if he personally, and
deliberately had and (quite unofficially)
endowed the object with magical powers.
I'm out gathering nicknames. All too
frequently you overestimate your personal
powers. There is no truth in beauty, no
beauty in truth. It does not exist.
Only the lie persists. The sound so loud
you can't hear screaming. I'd call that
an extreme of some sort. Listen to the
rodents bearing news. Life was, death is
a brief flirtation with existentialism.

THERE COMES SUCH A MOMENT OF FORGETFULNESS.

If I'm not mistaken, I think I saw, now
it was getting toward dark, I think I
saw a unit of clowns go by. Camouflaged
like they were trying to get through a
circus unnoticed. Oh, yeah, fully armed.
One of 'em was juggling shrunken heads.
There didn't really seem to be a captain
clown, but a couple of the tougher looking
ones had strings of clown noses around
their necks and I saw a few orange scalps.
They mighta been Koreans. Grey trees,
little yellow leaves, the smell of song.
Often enough, I can erase the big stuff
and only the details remain. Rather
interesting, seeing a landscape with
seeds, a blade of grass here and there.
And mostly, the invisible implications.
The splendor of inspiration. The things
you cannot see are so often the great
scenes of all time. Though let's not
be stupid. I like looking at stuff, too.

TEARS ARE NO SIGN OF DEEP FEELING.

I came up to a field, with a blackred glow.
A pretty well kept garden of lightbulbs
that looked like black lightbulbs. I
mean black tomatoes. Something about
light. I can sleep right through it.
Let me at the clouds. The dusk, the rain
moving in. Give me the thick stiff
flexible night. Begin thinking. Try
to recall every detail of an hour of your
life in five minutes. There feels like
something hanging off my head. Especially
in the wind. Big strips and flaps of
memory leather. A rather patient storm
hovered seven miles away, in uncharacteristic
equanimity in what resulted in a most
propitious delay. Time to check things.
I'm suffering from mass individual
confusion. I have a bullet-proof heart.

I have been physically altered. By a nearly perfect change of inner head. I have asked the inside of my face to check on things for me. The anger was channeled the wrong way, to the powerless. The black outfit with trousers, a swarm of sunshine. Little black dreams. They moved fast. Like the things you see when you're not well. We followed the afterblack. We saw a small cave. It smelled like a hidden pass. Trying to greet every tree fairly and eagerly. And the sun came through like a running sore. Hey, hold on, I'm the guy with the heart of gold. How did you get through the rain without getting wet? Oh now, you wouldn't want me to give away my only secret.

"HOW EXCESSIVELY PROVOKING!"

They were a great army. Quality you
could smell. Men. They were different
because they were not quite the same.
But they were the same because of the
fact they were the same thing. Splain
that once. I surmise, some resign their
positions as humans with a silly smile.
When they die, I mean. Others call down
the gods. The real men, the men who
live in history, before us, as lions,
or heroic defiant maniacs, they went down
too. They went smiling and spitting.
Better than the men who did not expect
to die, or did not particularly want to.
Some of these men are warriors when they are
dressed for it. Others are not. Some
remain mayors, butchers, boys. There
should be a solution. This should be one.
I stink, therefore I am. I understand.

IT IS HUMILIATING, UNBEARABLE TO BE BAFFLED LIKE THIS.

Another string of lies you would like to set off under me. I don't think, I don't think much about death anymore. Yours or mine. I just figured it out, well, a few months ago, it's almost impossible to live forever. Some attained peaks of magnificence during those years that were never again reached. I had a nice dream about night. I sat there and became symbolic. I'm afraid to open this big box. The unearthing of Satan's lips. Stupid as thunder, throat was violently dry. I'm not up for it. So picture this; I just want gifts I can eat or burn or throw away. May I faint with honor? I thought, therefore I am. There are exactly a million questions we should not ask. I keep an empty gun in my desk. I keep a loaded one in my right eye. Just so tired, I just want to lie down in the rain and go out sleeping. Away. Laid there like a wounded boot. I must have been raised by deer or snakes or some beast. I need to go live with the monkey people. Getting magic again. Put some water in my eyes, be able to see deep again. Abrupt increase in enigma, the creamy soot of evening. A nice lace lizard. Handcuffed by dizziness. Considering how little we know, it is remarkable how we dream so much of it. There are a lot of things we don't even know about (can't even imagine) never will think of, won't ever believe. Are we doing this because we want to or because we get to? Dress us all up in little bowties, and give us little dress up guns, red, yellow, blue. Beautiful little children to lead the way with flowers, chimes, tambourines and oatmeal box drums. Then mow us all down.

III. THE CHARM IS SNAPPED.

Kill dark.
Bring me dark.
Bring me dark's head.

THE DOLL.

The doll goes back a long way in time.
Children and adults both had dolls.
Men and women. The children played
with theirs. The adults used them
differently. Some were to comfort.
Some for companionship. Some were used
to frighten. Some were messengers. I
used a thick pack of letters. That was
my doll. I checked on it as often as
I could. I slept with it. I gave it
to a friend to hold when I got shot. Then I
gave it to another friend when he got shot.
Another composite. It is a wonderful
world. Exceedingly complete. A few
omissions. They are completely objective
are they not? One man's war is another's
war. One war can be one man's fruition,
and another man's early end. The same
thing can be not that thing. Could one
say that one man's what is another man's
what? Are we talking about one day that
can be glory and despair? Would you be
willing to help me out on this? You
can pit yourself against many things.
I guess you can create your own adversary.

It can be the obvious ones that you can't
control. You must try to rid yourself
of those, through the obvious methods.
Like bombs, bullets, poison and fire.
But what if you choose time? The fury
of baffled dreams. On some of those days
I become a rattlesnake. One day I was a
dead Apache. Powerful with his history.
Powerful in the memories of those who
knew him. If you are in more memories
do you exist more? Waking up next to a
water buffalo's eye. Waking next to a
dead kid's life. Felt like I was in the
Neverglades. Thousands of tiny, flightless
zebras. Hornets from hell. Listen.
With a fresh ear. You will hear the
fresh sounds. Now open up your
good eye. I think the danger increases
with the piety. So this slimey, smiley
angel comes down. Slinking through the
clouds. Lands and walks, floats, or
whatever they do, over to my bunker.
"Heard the news, you'll be home for Christmas."
Oh, you're the asshole that spreads those
rumors, and I put a round where his black
heart should have been. A guy can't look
naive all his life. All his natural life.
Ever feel inappropriate? I'm flying away
now, to become purely sane.

TOO MUCH REALISM.

You know, if there was someone taking
pictures, it would be nice to take a
picture of him so he'd have a picture, so
if one guy could turn around in a fight
and take a picture of the photographer,
and maybe a combat artist could sketch
that, and somebody else could photograph
the combat artist sketching, maybe
somebody could throw a cheap camera over
and up to the N.V.A. and he could take a
picture or two of us taking pictures and
he could start that going among his gang,
and then I don't know what else.

158.

War widow. From nag to riches.

159.

The battleness.

160.

You know, this DOVE OF PEACE is getting awfully old. I'm not sure she could fly if she had to.

GONE.

Sitting under the moon in that weird blue light. I watch the old river go by. Funny how it can go and stay at once. Oh, oh. This is new. The moon is going down, the river getting smaller, really small, small as a bug.
Two moons, one up, one down.
Off it goes. Small as a pinhole, gone, out like a light.
one gone moon
two gone moon
one dark river
one black path
one long dark mind
alone in the dark
River is gone
gone with the light
path is gone
world is gone
I'm gone.

DOES IT MATTER?

Wend my way sounds better than just walking, doesn't it? Strolling much better than humping. But, then, we have plenty of euphemisms in war already.

161.

There's a little terror in my pants.

TOMBSTONE.

I am often asked; well, what are you going to do now?

162.

A little glimpse at a man who limps.

163.

Reknew.

MISSION IN AKSHUN.

Seems like a lot of people on the streets and in the shopping malls and in the bars are still missing in action.

RIV U LETS.

The rain washed out our spot so deep, it looked like we were sleeping on a very upset guy's forehead.

THE WOMAN.

Why scrape for a better image? She was an old bird.

TOMBSTONE.

It's never over, is it? Nothing's done.

164.

Snotty little lieutenants.

AGREE.

Well, you call me shit-leg.
Alright, no-arm, crow-eye?

NOT ME.

Didn't think this
would ever happen
to me.
Did you? Did you?
Look at me. Did
you ever think that
would happen to me.
Tell me the truth.
Do I look like
it would have happened
to me. I never thought
so. Fooled me. Screwed me up,
took me by surprise. I didn't
see it coming. I never thought
about it. Really didn't.
Never happen to me–
nope, not me
not me
never happen to me.

FEELS RATHER GOOD.

It feels so good
when I scream.
I scream in the day
right when I wake.
It seems to twist
the world when I scream.
I know it twists me.
It hurts all the way
up from my chest to
my head.
I broke a dog the other
day.
I knocked down some
trees.
I'm getting mail now
I could hire myself out
it's a personal thing.
I scream for myself
out of hate, just for fun,
to break things, to forget,
to pretend. I scream, as a ploy.
I give screams to friends.
I'm saving a big one for a special
occasion, but on the last day of earth
I'll be respectfully mute.

JUST ASKIN'.

The sounds of birds
hitting the windows.
Who'd a thought I'd die so young?
The crash of trees crumbling
spinning first like barber poles
then crumbling like cake
in piles at their own feet.
Who'd a thought I'd die so young?
The splash of water against
the rocks
shattering up and over like
glass.
Broken water— what a thought.
Who'd a thought I'd die so young?
Who'd a thought I'd live that long?
Who'd a thought I'd die that way?
Who'd a thought so far away?
So why did it happen,
so who's to blame
I wanted to be from some place
I wanted to go somewhere.
So I heard the sounds
of birds flapping around
like a storm in my ear.
Then I heard some trees
falling apart.
And I saw bright chips of
water bright and loud.
There was much more
but these were the main events
I witnessed
when I died quite young.

165.

What drives you on drives me away.

DEER HUNTING.

I dreamed I had some gold buck's teeth.

166.

'splain that once, please.

FLIES.

Goddamn flies. I could say more.

167.

Oh, treats from the far east.

SHELLSHOCK.

There's a weird piece in him. A sound, roughly corresponding to our word ARGH.

NOT YET.

As yet, there is no truly polite term
for "you lousy motherfucker."

re: TIME.

A day is a long time to not see somebody.

HOPELESS HOPE.

The hope of no hope.

TOMBSTONE.

There were some faithful and true
walking into this
godless mess.

TO THE POINT.

Almost immediately, not quite yet, not
right now.

CORRECTION.

Making the most of in~~n~~accuracies.

THEY WOULDN'T ALLOW ME TO BE A BUDDHIST.

So what's close? Presbyterian? Fine.

168.

Lessnessness.

169.

A bowl of contradictions.
Eluded imagination.
Remorseless reiteration.
I had a point to make, it was quite a sight,
Jesus.

170.

Have you read Siddhartha?
I don't know for sure, what did he write?

171.

Pretty soon you'll have a gun in your hand, blowing your own nose off.

HAPPY VALENTINE'S DAY.

I'm not sure about this.
Why'm I tellin' you this?
I am having a hard time,
a very hard time.
I believe in things that
are not true.
I trust people who do not
exist.
I plant flower seeds in salt.
I send letters to the moon.
I bite off the heads
of dogs on the street.
I try to do it all,
I succeed despite the odds.
I persist in weirdness.
Why am I telling you this?

YOU HAVE A CHOICE.

onesty, oneste, aneste, anesti, onesti,
honysty, honysti, onysti.

POEM.

I didn't have poetry for it then.

TOMBSTONE.

Frame this.
Frame these dates.

TOMBSTONE.

Look, in your cupped hands,
look in your cupped hands.

TOMBSTONE.

Oh, you figure it out.

HANDCUFFED IN THE VAGUE.

Every creature there in the jungle, with a
tongue, sat up and stared at the moon.
Each one cried out, tongue flapping, little
reflections on them. From the moon, it
looked like the biggest city on earth.
The gleaming tongues flicking like light
flickering. After awhile, I realized
nobody was who they were at first. They
were composite humans. Created through
their own preferences. Sometimes an
innocent would be molded with strong
outside influences. Not his fault. It is
easy to change some people. Too often
for the worse. An undeniable history, a
reproachable future. He had a big grim
on his face. An unapproachable future.
Put an end to life. Like an old curse,
you erode the soul and ultimately kill.
When you see a bullet go through your
best friend's eye, you do not believe in
god very much. I am living because I made
it so.

All the hands that were lost found
each other and united. I hope the world
does not catch on fire. On behalf of all
of us involved, I thank you. And will
accept, as emissary, your thanks, and
distribute it evenly among them. You are
always an ex-soldier who is doing something
else. If you're not going to listen to
anybody, you have to listen to somebody.
I was brought up in the states, then, of
course, I was brought down. Dead birds
and a bagful of humidity. You know there
are no geese there. No Canada geese, no
white ones. Why then do I hear the geese
cries, the geese cry, a goose cry. Saw a
white one, too. Seeing with two left eyes,
there was a huge black bird jumping from
tree to tree skreeking and throwing things
with his wings.

He was laughing madly. It looked like
he was wearing a lot of rings on his feet.
It was a first class tantrum, fit or
seizure. The raven maniac. It was a
still life on fire. There are no
people in the painting. If there were, they
too, would be afire. As it is, only the
trees, the ground, the big plants, the
small ones beneath, the bugs, the birds,
some flying, some crawling, even the rocks
and dirt. And there's a chipmunk calling
through the flame. Help me, I'm
grotesquely out of place. Why are they
afraid of us? We're just going to rub
them out. It's cool. We all return to
the soil. We crumbled down the hill. Since
fate has brought us together, should
we not make the best of it? Spending
far too much time thinking about
sex. Rarely a thought crosses the mind
without a hook-up to lust. Just walking
around collecting dust. Unanswerable
fascinating secrets of the earth. On
ambush, what a relief. It was just a
bunch of sparrows. Tempestuous relief.
There is not much of a view from here.
I mean from inside this hole, I mean.
A terrible hemorrhage of imagery. Now
I know I am a fearful man.

TOMBSTONE.

Nothing to be afraid of.
Nothing of which to be afraid.

TOMBSTONE.

Involved in a long grim drag.

THE EVENIN'S COLOR.

Dark grey, a little bluen red.

COINCIDENCE.

I took off my shirt and jammed it down
my pants. Protection from a kick or
a knife. As it happened, he hit both.

DEAR BOB.

You've probably heard those horror stories about venereal disease you can get over here. Some stories go so far as to say that some guys get it so bad, they ship you to the Phillipines forever and tell your folks that you're on a secret mission. Then they say that your balls get so big that you have to carry them around in a wheelbarrow. That's bullshit. You can carry them around fine in a newspaper bag, or a pail. Then you have a hand free. Secret mission my ass. We don't do anything here. Movies and comic books. It's really easy.

DID IT, EH?

Well, well, so you really did it.
You sat around and pulled out your
eyes. Now what will you do?
Your money will sleep forever.
With your luck the world becomes
prettier just so you can't see it.
Well, well, the better for some
others who will appreciate it.
You must get a new dignity,
or is that a new identity?
Change your voice, cut your
hair, maybe cut off your hands
so you won't hurt yourself anymore.

REMEMBER, THIS IS A MELODIC FICTION.

A snake curled up and purred along
with me. (Beneath that streak of Blue
below that high long cloud
under that big light mood
in the shadow of that deep sky cut.
The exit wound we often wait for.)

A LIST FROM THEN.

Is your life as sharp now
as your memory of then is now?
Positive about everything.
But oh so wrong about it all.
1. The road mistaken.
2. The road of glass.
3. The bridge of dreams.
4. The path of fire.
5. The lake of thick snake soup.
Raising some weird air.
Stirring up some.

NOW.

The lies must stop now. It takes such a short time to forget what really happened. History can be altered in the good name of salving the wounds.

172.

It is hard to see my part.

173.

It could be said that there is a mystical element to war. An unaccountable, and originless energy that pervades those who are willing or oblivious recipients. A takeover that can last any length of time.

174.

I feel so badly for the, well, the dorks that had to go. Unless of course NOW they're glad they went. We all know that unwilling participation sometimes proves to be the greatest experience of all time.

175.

If you know everything, you'll get a chance to use something, sometime.

THE KING OF SADNESS.

He wore a crown of frowns, bejewelled with pretty blue tears. Some borrowed from his friends, others found on the roads. Some he would take right out of the newspaper. There are millions of them everywhere. These tears are everywhere. A king with no policy. Except to remain unhappy forever. A living royal reminder that woe exists. I wonder now, drinking from the bowl of light. My head felt like it was drifting. At the instant precisely when you slide fast into loose gravel on your bike. If you pull back too quickly, you will go insane. If you wait, over you go. And that's for sure. Thoughts came too fast. Like a game of slapjack. By the time the game is nearly done, everybody's hands are flapping in the pile. It is a mess. Your hands hurt, and the cards are all bent. So it is with thought.

WHAT SAD WORDS THOSE ARE.

Standing near, you can grab it with your hand. That thick shadow. We cast very important shadows. Imperfect shadows, pinpricks of light in their heads, and around the hearts. Too pretty to kill. Isn't that an odd thought? With his camouflage, he looked just like a huge fuckin' leaf, or a rare butterfly with a rifle. The pervading spirit at the time must have been a clown. Or should that be the presiding spirit must have been a clown. Or the prevailing spirit at the time was clownlike. A real bush league diety. He was brilliantly demented. He was not a man, he was a creature.

WITH A VIVID THRILL.

Your mind can block out many things when you do not have one. I have heard of a thief of sadness. Moving at inspirational speed. In and out of firelight. Some doubt. I don't know what I'm going to do. I don't know where I'm going. Through the herbage, planting henbane, and covering up our tracks. We don't want the credit for that. The way the wind blows the trees, it makes them look alive. We first suspect before we doubt. Is there a difference? A bundle of noises on the side of the path. Little skriks and little skraks, hundreds of wind-up teeth from Taiwan. Their fear officer really had an imagination. A very special job. Funny sounds out there. If I had to explain how they were, I would say to ask a group of first grade children to read license plates aloud for about six years with only short breaks for whiskey. That is what those sounds were like.

FEELS VERY BITTER AGAINST THE DEAD MAN.

Overcoat on, windy. The day the Big
general said the enemy was in his place was
the day he was in my place too. The
company was nearly wiped out. Terry
got killed right next to me. He never
did get that new surfboard. So I asked
him what he thought about the enemy being
in its place. He was dead, so he didn't
answer. But, I think, with his sense of
humor, he would have said: "Whose place is
this anyway, whose woods are these, I think
I know." Wouldn't you think so? Note to
the mountain. I consider the rejection
of my life as a gift to you the ultimate
insult. It is clear that you need more
time for self-examination. I herewith
withdraw my generous petition. However,
if you wish to reconsider, I will be residing
in my own imagination. You may find
me there, or inquire at the desk.
I am often of a contrary nature. Out.

THE AWE SYNDROME.

Green night, the storm was a wonderful
monster. I had the great creeps. With
snatches of memory I built a nightmare,
then tore it apart bit by bit the next
night and had a fairly snappy dream.
The subtractive method works for awhile.
A shortage or something. A very light
red. Not a pink. This distinction must
be made. Those few flowers are a bit short
on red. And those are underrated thistles.
A terrific lavender, perfect white tops.
I am sitting alone among blind, sightless
fools. I have recently been elected
their leader. As from time, I got
half an answer, scars on the air. Was
I to read and interpret time? Was a
man like me expected to interpret these
skyroglyphics? They kept shifting around
so I'm sure the meaning changed every
few minutes. And my credibility as a
translator was rapidly going to hell.

THE SNARE IS TOO PLAINLY SET.

Busting apart like a talking parrot in a
shooting gallery. It was a bird from
a proper home. No crackers for this
joker. Polly want some glue and a front
row seat in heaven. Polly want a street
lined with gold. A noticeable tilt, eh?
This walking gives a fella a real sore
back. Sort of like doing a lot of dishes
or hovering over jewelry counters.
Depending what was in your mouth when
you were born. I just could not believe
it. You'll find it tough to swallow too,
I'm afraid. I got lost one night and
walked all night. At first light I
spotted a road sign. Well, I read a
little French. I was three kilometers
from Dienbienphu. The sign said you are
here. Well, I knew that. Many other
informational signs were absent. Like
why, for how long, what do I do next?
I got the feeling that the other side
of the sign would read: now you're not.
For a second, whatever that is, I felt
free as an ego. This could be a case of
hysteron proteron, the later earlier, the
latter first. Well, I din't want to be
neither. Just because it's esoteric,
doesn't mean I won't use it. Is there
anything else I should know. Is it advisable
to provide additional material? You have
to remember a lot to be a grown-up. We must
not allow cynicism to prevent the joy in
simple things. Some aspects of the life I know.

FUNERAL DIRGE.

Last chants.

TOMBSTONE.

He was a child of his own mind. Sounds like something somebody fancy might have said.

PATROL.

We've got 35 minutes before we go. We're getting ready. The darker it gets, the darker we are. We can't talk again until morning. These may be our last mumbles. Break out the camouflage. Make ourselves invisible. Make ourselves silent.

A SMALL CHAPTER ON BEES.

It was such a queer day. Hot with rain.
Then the wind came in and brought in some
dust. Where that came from we couldn't
say. Way north maybe. But one of us
noticed it when it was a mile or two
away. A black thing in the air. Never
had seen anything like it so we just
said look at that thing. It was like
looking at an octopus for the first time.
Then more of us came around and started
staring. It came closer. Or it was
getting bigger. It was hard to say.
You know how the stories about how the
buffalo covered the plains for miles,
or for as long or far as you could see
sounded unreal? Nothing's that large.
Well, this black thing covered the sky
like it <u>was</u> the sky.

Then we noticed the sound. It was like
a telephone line in the country. A
loud humm. It went with the black thing
very well. The shape changed slightly.
Like a fast moving cloud. Little tails
dropping off here and there. A streamer
going up, then rejoining the body. We
knew we were seeing something rare.
Something great. It came straight for us,
and in seconds it was on us. We were it.
All the bees there ever were were there.
Our swearing exceeded the humm it brought.
But only for a second. We barely had
time to get our weapons. We grabbed
everything. We grabbed anything. Guns,
clothes, some threw food. We swung shovels.
We got our rifles loaded. Shooting
back at the bees, 130 rifles blazing
away. A thick yellow ooze coming from
the sky. Slowly, the air dripping.

Then it was hand to hand. First rifle
butts and bayonets. It turned to hands and
swatting, crushing, then as a last resort
we just kept clapping, the little fuckers
dropping, some winged, some dead. They
were just too close. They came in fast
and often. We were all hit pretty bad.
Some of us went blind. Some of the others
were so swollen they were not the same
person, except inside. And, now that I
think about it, the stings did get in
there, too. A fight like that goes
pretty deep. We sat back with the same
relief and horror and sense of winning
and escape, as if we had just wiped out
a company of men. Somebody joked later.
It was a poor attempt. I finished a few
off with a book by Nietzsche. No survivors.

They called us Bee Company after that.
Fuckers. We lost some men in that fight.
We never capped on the motorpool for all
the guys they ran over. Or the cooks
who choked on their own cooking. Yeah,
so we joked about a couple of officers
who died screwing. But then that's
privilege of rank. Afterwards, those
of us remaining walked around putting the
sword to the wounded. Stepping on bees.
The little snap, not quite like twigs.
Almost like frail glass. Maybe more
like ice cracking in that cool drink, eh?

TOMBSTONE.

We will never be the same.

TOMBSTONE.

Dried arrangements.

LONG DISTANCE LOVER.

Even through the letter, a hateful
document, she put out my eyes with
her stare. Her breath smelled strongly
of dreams. Smelled like smoke, whiskey,
and sleeping men. We ended our love with
a preposition. The fountain pen was bleeding.

WAR TROPHY.

Put his teeth and eye in a jar of bull
piss. They shined like a star in the
morning.

176.

There are many people whom one could
term el vicarioso, or, in turn, la
vicariosa.

177.

Mulgering.

THE COLONEL WITH THE SILVER STAR.

Why should you get the credit while the
others did the work? You were in a
helicopter, remember?
Oh, that's right. Here, give it to somebody
who got his lips shot off. After all, I've
had it since 1967 anyway. Somebody else's turn.

TOMBSTONE.

Friendship, you mock the word. You
are a bully. You are cheap and spiteful.

178.

I saw a bird swing down to catch a floating
insect. It was good to see that the dead
were of some use.

179.

Hey, what are you shooting at?
I saw something move.
Hey, everything's moving.

TOMBSTONE.

I'm in a pit of battlesnakes. Stay
away.

180.

With brown grass for protection,
carrying our rifles, god, weren't
we men. Things haven't changed
since then.

OPEN WINDOW.

I must keep the doors open for contradictions.
If I don't, I may die of strangulation,
or frustration. I must remember to open
the windows during a terrible storm.

NOVEMBER 15.

Hold your fire.
Got something in my eye.

181.

So who gets the royalties for Mein Kampf?

182.

Feather in my cap. I am still looking for my Viet Nam d'plume.

183.

Think of this one. We were in a war run by Madmen, Commies and Teenagers.

MAYBE NOTHING.

No more lovers
no more nothing
no more maybe
only we who choose
to speculate
can choose
to do no more
to see no more
except that's
not possible either
because the eyes
never close
the love never stops
the answers always come
the blood is always
there
the hell remains
and, too, the storm.
No more lovers
almost nothing
maybe
maybe
I hope
I hope
I hope
I hope
I hope
I hope
I hope
I hope
I hope
I hope

IT'S QUIET IN THERE.

My head feels like it is in a tin can. I have been thinking again. Planning things. Like what to read, where to go, and who to see. What to buy, who to be, and why. You know, there are no answers. Even to the simple problems. I mean, no perfect answers. Especially to the simple questions.

BUT HOW ODD, HOW COLD, THAT COULD
NEVER BE.

Beyond their thought, out in the green
zone, off in the sandstorm. The dead are
beyond their own thought, not ours.
Out there in the dead place, the grey
place; they sit or float, victims of
our imaginations. Products of our whims.

Way way out, up and out, steamy regions,
cold, they say. The joint where the
sane don't go. But I don't buy that.
Save some room. It's a long flat place,
isn't it, flat and long, with a spot of
orange here and there. A patch of orange
hate.

I ate a spicy woman. I wrote myself
into a dream. But there my control
ceased. The night head took over.
I drove everywhere I had ever been.
God, what a trip that was. I painted
myself into a corner using every color
I had ever seen. The painting was of a
dream. Landscapes appeared at random,
though I knew all of them.

When the painting was over the dream vanished. God, what a painting that was. My pillow is still stained deep with most of the colors. I built a room with many rooms in it. They were bigger than the room they were in. That's exactly how I feel. I never feel smaller than the world I am in. I became friends with a stranger lately. Which one of us created the new friend. We both want credit. We both have shown immense power.

Like in Mondrian's squares, maybe when it's done, you'll feel like an early chrysanthemum. If the air's like this forever, then I'll stand by the door forever. I don't like this field. I don't like the sounds. Too many high noises. Do you hear the high notes? I can't seem to breathe. I open my mouth and inhale a vine. I am attached to the ground. I am anchored hard. Will I root like Mondrian's flower. Shallow and pale?

IT HURTS ME STILL.

I have been poisoned. I went to the
airport to throw up. I drank too much
green whiskey. I sweat until I fall down.
I'm cold on a hot day. I don't know
the people I'm meeting. I hate them
instantly. I'm in a fast yellow car.
I am still quite ill. I'm sure I'll
die soon. Put me away somewhere. Stop
my heart. Please stop my heart. My arms
are heavy. They don't move. I have
been poisoned, as I've said. I've
got to get out of it if I can. I'll
get out of it what I can. Maybe I'll
write a book about what it's like to die.

TOMBSTONE.

Let time pass
one day goes
comes another

DAK TO PART I

The sun came up. Sounded like rattlesnakes.
Once again, I found myself in the forest
Situation. The dawn, coming once each day,
Is beautiful. The largest star I've ever
Seen, hanging midway in the sky every
Morning. Wading through time. And I've
Got this crazy bitch of a river running
Next to me. There was just too much
Beauty. I could not take it all. We all
Have different capacities. Some of you
Were there. Some of you don't care, that's
Cool. A bruised mind. A formerly impeccable
Memory, now flawed. It is here, (in my
Dream, in my work) I am in my beloved
Milieu. My simple eyes saw one thing.
The complex eyes, with mind attached, saw
Many things. Some things could not
Even be seen, due to the manyness of them.
I saw a Great Blue Regret feeding the other
Day, drinking deeply from a clearly marked
Pool of poison. Unrest Blue. I feel
Kind of lost, kind of empty almost.

A contrary geography, lush and naked.
There is always a great distance between
The foot of a hill and the peak. If
Indeed, hills have peaks. Just the other
Night I was everywhere at once. My hands
Were smiling. Incredibly silent, A Deliberate
Act, I'd guess. Mute with purpose.
Let me blend into the night with my dark
Thoughts. I'm not used to thinking this
Way. It was grey and cold. Then it
Became beautiful. People disappeared
One by one. Then in groups. Ten or
Twelve in Fargo. Fifteen in Moscow.
It keeps going on. Newspapermen kept
Hard at work, dedicated to the beauty
Of the story. Artists recorded it in
Paint, word, and song until they vanished
As well. Their pens dropping to the
Floors of their workrooms with senseless
Clatter. I, of course, was the last to
Go. And you have not heard a word of
What I have said. Woke up in a bug's
Nest, pondering my own history. Mountains
In flames, men without names. Startled
By the sun, stunned by the moon. So,
Inevitably, I returned to write this.
I feel kind of lost, kind of empty almost.

So, we took a little walk, we thought we
Could take it. Walked in the hills, most
Didn't make it. Up in the hills, dead in
The hills, deep in the hills, the hills
Of Dak To.

A little place in the hills. Come up
For a few thrills. A wooded wonderland
Called Dak To.

Take a little trip, where do we go?
Oh, up in the hills, the hills of Dak To.

We goin' for a little climb. Bring your
Guns and bring some wine, we gon' have a
Real good time.

Trade some lead and have a few laughs.
A little place in the hills, come up
For a visit. A wooded dream called Dak To.

Take a little trip, what do you know?
Oh, we're gonna get killed in the hills
Of Dak To. Wanna get killed in the hills
Of Dak To.

1.
Hey ho, let's go.
Up to the hills, the hills of Dak To.

2.
Hey ho, let's go.
Gonna get killed in the hills of Dak To.

3.
Hey, ho, let's go.
Wanna get killed in the hills of Dak To.

4.
Hey ho, let's go.
Up to the hills, the hills of Dak To.

5.
Grab some pot.
Get some wine, we're gonna have a real good time.

PART II

Maybe our burial began the day we put
Our guns off safety. This giant arm
Came out of the sky and drew us as we
Were fighting. I was not seeing god, or
Some huge Cartoonist. It was a beautifully
Done pencil drawing of a hand, and we were
Being drawn by it. In the same style as
The hand was done in. Brilliantly, and
In better detail than we really were.
There we were, running up a hill, running
Into death against our will. The air
Was filled with shots and shouts, and the
Million year old sound of battle. Screaming
Commands, questions, pleas, I wonder how
You say, "What the fuck's goin' on?" in
Babylonian or Incan. The thing is, no
Matter what weirdness you just saw, it
Will become weirder and weirder. It is
The natural order. You expect it. Weirdness
Is normal. If things were normal, it would
Be weird. If you saw the weirdest thing
You ever saw today, tomorrow you would
Expect, you could count on, you would have
No choice but to see and do something
Weirder. You would be helpless to prevent
It. You would be crushed if it didn't
Happen. And if it didn't, that would be
So fuckin' weird, it would do.

It wasn't so real as you'd think, getting
Shot at would be. One minute you'd be
Standing up. And the next second, a
Guy would be dead on the ground. Like
Magic. Not like in the movies, or the
Great war books, which allowed you to
Picture the beautiful, smokey battle.
The men, enemies and friends, dropping
Picturesquely in a slow, agonizing dance.
The dance of death. Every corpse had a
Nijinsky in him. Not in reality. In
Reality, men fall and go blank. Some
With sick, Goddamnit looks on their faces.
Some twisted and turned, looking for
A good place to fall. Absurd acts, absurd
Words, and even thoughts are the defense
Of the otherwise confused or speechless
Person. I swear I saw a tree bend over
To shield a man. The tree paid dearly.
Famous last words. A beautiful sight.
If you could just slow it down to catch
More detail. How quickly men fall slowly.
How slowly the men run quickly. A man
Is dead before the sound hits him. You
Can hear yourself die, by the way. I
Heard it, and I was told, too. Of course,
A dead man told me.

Slaughtered in a rockery, a regular
Shangri la Del Muerte. Skulls poised
With jaws open, arms out, stretched in a
Mock opera.
He is no longer exist.
His no existence
He's no
The moonlight fell across my chest like a
Fluttering sash. When he fell, the sash
Tumbled down the hill. Let some stranger
Carry him off, a stranger had killed him.
Strange thought. As a friend, I should
Have done it. If he'd been living, I
Would have done it. Carried him to Algeria.
I do not want to be remembered for that.
I still shake my head like a dog with a
Sore ear, side to side, whining, trying
To throw those thoughts out. Hoping
They'll fly out and land on the sidewalk
Where I could stamp them to death with
My cloven hoof.

THE ESSENCE COLLECTOR.

There was one job that was forgotten.
The Essence Collector. A man or woman,
A child could not do it. Finely dressed,
With very well-made bags, made of some
Fine cloth that wears well, full of excellent
Boxes, engraved with outstanding moments
In the person's life. The Collector
Would walk slowly, snapping essences
From the dead. The sooner the better.
The battlefield would be howling. The
Collectors would come by, maybe in squad
Size, sometimes larger groups would be
Needed. Their little boxes snapping
And clicking, and sliding shut. Capturing
The blurring blue light that was living
Moments earlier. After the battle, they
Look for the lost dying, or the lost
Dead, to find the lost essence, hoping
It hung around long enough to put away.
Some refuse to come, of course, and bounce
Off trees in their panic to escape. Like
Non-lunatics running from the nut-house
Guards. But see, here is where it gets
Confusing. I don't know what they do
With them. It's not like a bug collection.
Or urns of ashes. And, they are not
Just boxes of memories. We have plenty
Of those. No, this is big.

It is said the dead live in our memories.
So to speak, in a sense, in a manner of
Speaking, figuratively, that we keep
Them alive. But what when <u>we</u> die?
Does the memory die with us, or do the
Others inherit the memory of the newly
Dead? No, that's too much to ask of
Anyone. One memory is plenty for most
Of us. And many of us try to erase the
Ones we have. See, that's why we get
The Essence Collectors. This job could
Go to Asians. They have a strength in
That area that westerners don't have. Or
Maybe our very old. It would be quite
A sight to see qualified, agile old
People carefully doing this important work.

BULLETS.

Some say they move fast as lightning.
Others quicker than thought. That's
Pretty fast. I say they were always
There. Stationary <u>and</u> moving at incredible
Velocity. There are some things we just
Cannot prove. So, I might be right.

PART III

Absurd acts, absurd words, and even thoughts
Are the defense of the confused or otherwise
Speechless person. Surprise me. I don't
Begrudge them their lives. It's just
That they don't <u>know</u> anything. Hey, I'm
Too damn aware. Dying's not easy when
You know it's there. O.K. then, life
Is optional. I don't know if that means
That death is optional or not. I feel
Kind of lost. Kind of empty almost.
Somehow blundered into death as we bungled
Through life.

PART IV

I think the guys that worried the most
Got killed the most. "To live is sufficient
To conquer." Lying dead, punctured by
Shards of poetry. I can hate things now
For what they are, or for what they are not.
My simple eyes saw one thing. The complex
Eyes, with mind attached, saw many things.
Some things could not even be seen, due
To the manyness of them. There is a
Moment when the truth is so clear and clean
It's stunning. Then, just as suddenly, it's
Gone. I hate many things we were taught
To love. Do not ask me what those are.
You really do not want to know.

After the fire, we sifted through. And
Against our combined wills, found what we
Had dreaded. Hundreds of the peacocks,
Living only hours ago, lay melted, smouldering.
An immense, wax-like, purple pool, the faces
Still intact. The colors held on limply.
Ready to drop from their hosts. Will
The jungle hear our song? Will the bones
Of the dead say, "It's o.k. now... I'm
Not angry anymore?" Or will they feel
The way I would feel, and invent a hell
And send me to it? Make arrangements
Or come to terms with all the spirits.
Even the ones you don't believe in.
How long would it take us to make a wreath
To stand for every dead one? Do we even
Have the manpower? Of course. We'd give
The work to the Vietnamese in America.
We pay them to make their own memorials.
It is now, so many years later, that I
Regret not killing anyone. Or not knowing
How many I killed, or knowing so many
Who were killed, killed by the unknown.
Known by the killed. I can still run
Like the wind. Well, an older wind.
War improved me.

Part V

There is at least one of us still there.
Eating bananas and monkeys and snakes.
Going around confident with exertion.
Burying everybody he can find. Probably
Enlisted the aid of ghosts who could not
Get back. I wonder how ghosts get across
Oceans. I would think the wind would
Blow them apart. Or the rain would
Pack them down until they were just a thin
Film on the surface of the water, undulating
Like sunshine. Sending futile signals
To the living, who wouldn't know a signal
From a ghost from a hole in the ground.
A film too thin to be seen from the air
Anyway. A film too scary for sharks to
Attack. I think maybe it would be best
For the ghosts to stay there. Somebody
Knows what happened. I swear, it was so
Terrible, I'd recommend it to everyone.
So, inevitably, I returned home to write this.
I feel kind
Of lost
Kind of empty
Almost.

This first edition of WAR HANGOVER consists of 1500 copies. 250 copies in a limited edition are numbered, signed and hand colored by the author. Set in Bookman type by Byron and Dorie Higgin of the Clarkfield Advocate in Clarkfield, Minnesota. Printed on Wausau bond offset by Anvil Press in Millville, Minnesota.

Angel Wing Press
1987